CONFESSIONS OF A JACKBOY

Nicholas Lock

Lock Down Publications & Ca$h Presents

Confessions of a Jackboy

A Novel by *Nicholas Lock*

Nicholas Lock

Lock Down Publications
P.O. Box 944
Stockbridge, Ga 30281

Visit our website at www.lockdownpublica-
tions.com

Book interior design by: **Shawn Walker**
Edited by: **Nuel Uyi**

Stay Connected with Us!

Text **LOCKDOWN** to 22828 to stay up-to-date with new releases, sneak peaks, contests and more...
THANK YOU.

Submission Guideline

Submit the first three chapters of your completed manuscript to ldpsubmissions@gmail.com, subject line: Your book's title. The manuscript must be in a .doc file and sent as an attachment. Document should be in Times New Roman, double spaced and in size 12 font. Also, provide your synopsis and full contact information. If sending multiple submissions, they must each be in a separate email.

Have a story but no way to send it electronically? You can still submit to LDP/Ca$h Presents. Send in the first three chapters, written or typed, of your completed manuscript to:

LDP: Submissions Dept
Po Box 944
Stockbridge, Ga 30281

*DO NOT send original manuscript. Must be a duplicate. *

Provide your synopsis and a cover letter containing your full contact information.

Thanks for considering LDP and Ca$h Presents.

Acknowledgements

Everyone who worked on my book—from the typist to the editors—I appreciate you!

Rai'chell, lol! I told you, you should know I'd never thug you. I feel like we have an understanding that's beyond words.

Kiyyah, I appreciate you, little buddy. You been holding me down so it's only right that I hold you down when I come home.

Readers and fans—Without you, there's no book. Each time I pick up my pen, I have y'all in mind. I want to keep y'all on the edge of your seats and entertained throughout each book. I'm curious to know your thoughts and comments on this book or any of my books. You can send them to:

Nicholas Lock- 0932600
P.O Box 506
Maury, NC 28554

Nicholas Lock

Prologue

The story is called *Confessions of a Jackboy,* but I wasn't always a jackboy. My name is Face, by the way. Part of that is because I love *Scarface,* and the other part is because I have a scar on my face under my eye from getting stabbed, but that's a story for another time. So, before I take you on this ride and show you this jackboy swag, let me give you the rundown on how it all started—

"It should be against the law to be this goddamn sexy," I said, checking myself out in my nigga Murph's mirror.

"Face, get out the mirror and let's go," Murph said.

"We not leaving yet, it's only eight-thirty," my twin—Trip—said. "The only people that get to parties early are lames and thirsty ass niggas."

It was me, Murph and my identical twin: Trip. We were getting ready to go to a party in Oakdale that these redbones—Kay Kay, Tessa and Bria—were having. Murph was my day one nigga, besides my twin. If you saw me, you saw him; it was rare to see one without the other. At sixteen, Murph was the youngest while me and Trip were seventeen. Murph's mom was white and his pops was black, so he was one of them light-skinned niggas that stayed on his bougie light skin shit. Me and my brother were brown-skinned. All of us were 6'0 with waves. The only difference was, Murph kept his sides cut lower than the top. I must add that we were all certified hustlers! We had that gas and crack for the low.

"How much bread you got, Face?" Murph asked.

"It was a good week. You can't tell?" I pulled out two knots that equaled ten racks.

"You ain't said shit!" Murph said, pulling his money out, showing off the eighty-five hundred he had.

"Nigga, you not exempt! Run that!" I tapped Trip's pockets.

"Y'all ain't talking about shit," Trip continued talking on his phone.

"That got to be Carmen sexy ass he on the phone with," said Murph, causing Trip to look up. Trip was sensitive when it came to his girl.

Trip flashed what I guessed to be about fifteen racks, and went back to his conversation. He knew we would've stayed on his ass, so he got it out the way. Trip was the one that spent the least, so it didn't come as a surprise that he had the most money.

"Come on, let's bounce," I said, looking in the mirror one more time.

Since Oakdale was right next to our neighborhood, all we had to do was take the cut which was a little wooded area that separated the two neighborhoods. So we went ahead and walked. That way, we could smoke a blunt in peace.

"Pass the blunt, nigga!" Murph said to Trip.

Trip passed the blunt just as we got to the cut. We stopped in the cut to enjoy the weed, and a nigga stepped out from behind a tree.

"Damn, that shit smell like some fiyah! Y'all ain't got none for sale?" he asked.

"Hell nah," I told him. I had never seen him before.

"I ain't want none no way." *Click clack!* He pulled a gun out and cocked it back. "But I do want everything in your pockets."

"What!" Murph acted like he was ready to buck.

"Be a hero and they'll put your face on a shirt," the nigga said. In the end we got relieved of all our money and our jewels.

"What the fuck! We just got hit for almost thirty-five racks in ten minutes! We trapped all week long for that!" I snapped.

"That was all I had," Murph said with his head down.

Trip didn't say anything. He just started walking back home. As he walked home, the idea came to me that we'd chosen the wrong profession.

Now that you know all that, I can tell you the story of how I traded in my scale and work for a pistol and a ski mask. Enjoy the show!

Nicholas Lock

Chapter One

It had been eating at me that we'd been robbed of all our shit. I couldn't sleep the next few nights, and it didn't help that the football coach was on me and Trip's ass. We were seniors and captains of the Douglas Byrd football team. Trip was the starting quarterback, I played middle linebacker, and Murph played defensive end. Let our coach tell it we had major talent and could be playing in the NFL one day. That may have been true for Trip and Murph but not me. Not to say I couldn't, but I was a street nigga and I was thugging with no brakes. This was the life I chose and to be honest I loved it, the bullshit and all. I had come up with a plan, but I didn't know if Trip and Murph were going to go along with it or not. Me though, it wasn't a chance in hell I was about to sell a motherfucking thing.

"Trip, you riding with me or you riding the bus?" I asked. I was the only one with a car. Trip and Murph could've had one, but they would rather buy clothes and jewels.

"Nah, I'm going to take the bus. I need to holler at Tori-ano."

"A'ight, I'm gone, bye!" I yelled, walking out the house. I got into my white Cadillac Escalade Ext and peeled out. I had to go pick my lady up for school. Me and Rai'chell had been fucking around for the last few years. She was my bitch in every sense of the word. When Money Bag Yo made the song "Reflection", he was talking about Rai'chell. She was a reflection of me, and she was with whatever I was with. We stayed in basically the same neighborhood, so it only took a cool couple minutes for me to get to her house. My neighborhood was called Lafayette Village. It was a middle-class neighborhood that, from the outside looking in, you would take for a good place to live; that is, until the sun went down.

That's when all the trouble makers and knuckleheads came out. Rai'chell stayed on the other side, which was Ashton Forrest. The only thing that separated the two was Hope Mills Road. When I pulled up to Rai'chell's house, she was outside looking like a snack. Rai'chell was 5'2, cinnamon brown-skinned, with brown hair that fell to the middle of her back, and the type of body that would make you double take even if you were with your girl. She had freckles on her cheeks that added to her sex appeal.

"Hey, baby!" she said, hopping in the truck and kissing me on the lips.

"Sup," I said, checking her out. She was looking real edible in her Chanel pants and t-shirt. The pink outfit accentuated her full pink lips.

"Baby, are we going to the movies this weekend?"

"Maybe, it all depends—" I teased, already knowing that I was going to take her.

"On what?" She started to pout.

Oh yea, my bitch was bougie as fuck! She didn't do no fighting or anything that involved her to break a sweat. She had to have her nails and toes done. And her hair stayed done in the latest fashions.

"On how good you ride this dick." I grabbed her hand and put it in my lap.

"My period on, boo."

"Your mouth ain't." I unzipped my pants.

She mushed me in the head, and gave me some top the whole way to school. I filled her mouth with my kids just as I pulled into the school parking lot. She swallowed without giving it any thought. At sixteen, Rai'chell was already an expert in the sex department, courtesy of me. I was the only nigga that she'd ever been with, so I taught her all that I knew.

"Are you going to drive me home?"

"You know I got football practice," I said, getting my two hundred and twenty-five pound frame out of the truck. "Here, take my keys and don't wreck my shit, Chell." I used the nickname that I gave her.

"Okay!" She ran off to go show her homegirls she had the keys to my truck.

While Chell went to brag to her friends, I went to the cafeteria to get some breakfast. I got my tray, and went and sat in the booth by the window that we always sat at. Before I could take a bite out of my blueberry sausage, Murph and Trip walked up, arguing about football.

"Tom Brady is the goat," Trip said.

"Yeah, the greatest cheater of all time!" Murph countered.

"Don't forget about Belichick cheating ass," I added.

"Both of y'all are some full-blown haters," Trip said.

I went back to eating my food, while they went back and forth. I looked up from my tray as Kameesha walked up to our table. Me and Kameesha always flirted back and forth, but I never took it there because she was nowhere near as bad as Rai'chell in any category; nevertheless, she was one of those bitches that oozed sex appeal.

"Scoot over, nigga." She forced her way into the booth beside me.

I looked around to make sure Rai'chell wasn't anywhere around because I didn't have time to deal with the bullshit.

"What's good, Kameesha?" I asked, looking down at her exposed thighs.

Kameesha was built like a grown woman, but she was only seventeen. She had a yellow complexion, high cheekbones, shapely breasts, and what I believed to be a forty-inch ass. I'd been dying to get between her legs. I had heard from

15

numerous niggas that she had let them fuck. But we were in high school, and you know niggas tended to lie on their dicks back then.

"What's good is you *in* me," she said.

"Say no more, we gon' handle that at lunch, in the weight room, and you betta not be bullshitting," I told her.

"Okay," she beamed, getting up and strutting away.

"You stay getting yourself in some shit," Trip shook his head.

"What you talking about?" I was lost.

"Look," he nodded.

I turned to see my baby walking my way with fire in her eyes.

"Why was that dusty ass bitch all in your face?" She put her finger in my face.

"First off, take your fucking finger out my face and she was over here for Trip." I threw my twin under the bus.

"Don't get fucked up, nigga," she said. "Better yet walk me to my homeroom."

"Yo, I need to holler at y'all about some real shit later on," I said, walking off hand in hand with Rai'chell. After I walked her to her room, I stood at the door, then she looked askance at me.

"Aren't you gonna come inside?" Rai'chelle asked.

"Nah, I got to get back to Trip and Murph."

"Or you going to fuck that bitch in some goddamn tryst?"

"Come on! Don't be silly, Chell. I've got other fish to fry."

"If you say so. Just don't go about fucking behind my back. I ain't gon' condone that shit!"

"Noted. I gotta go now. Bye, babe." I left as she shut the door. My next port of call was the weight room, where I hoped to find Kameesha. I couldn't conceal my smile when I found her there.

"Why you still got them shorts on?" I asked, sitting on the weight bench inside the weight room.

"I didn't know you wanted them off," Kameesha said, wiggling out of them, showing me she didn't have on any panties.

"Bring yo' yellow ass here." I stepped out of the 501's I had on.

Me and Kameesha traded places with each other, putting her on the bench and me standing up.

"Hell nah, put this dick in ya mouth." She had laid back on the bench with her legs in the air.

"I don't know how to suck dick," she whined.

"You gon' learn today." I grabbed her by the back of her neck, and pulled her to me. Kameesha put my dick in her mouth, and started to bob her head back and forth.

"Just like that!" I coached her, and that seemed to send her into overdrive because she started to cut up.

"You like how I suck this dick?" Kameesha asked, jacking my dick.

I grabbed her head, and put my dick back in her mouth. "Ssss," I hissed, raising up on my toes.

Kameesha didn't miss a beat, as I started to rock my hips back and forth, which made me believe this wasn't her first time putting dick in her mouth. The only sound in the weight room was her slurping and sucking.

"I'm about to bust, Kameesha." I held her head, as I shot some of my kids into her mouth.

She swallowed every drop without gagging, letting me further know that she was all the way freaked out. And that was going to leave me with a clear conscience with what I was about to do.

"Lay down." I put a towel over her eyes and tied her hands to the weight bar.

"You a freak, Face," Kameesha said, as I finished tying her up.

"If only you knew."

I crept to the door, put my finger to my lips and let the entire football team in. I pulled my iPhone out and recorded it as the whole team took turns fucking Kameesha. She was going crazy the whole time, moaning and yelling my name like it was me fucking her. No matter what she said, I know she knew niggas was running a train on her. After everyone had a turn, I let them out and untied her.

"You fucked the shit out of me, boy," she said, putting her shorts back on.

I didn't say anything. I just shook my head and let her out. I sent the football team the video, and walked to my fourth period class with thoughts of how I was going to get Trip and Murph to jump on board with my new hustle.

Chapter Two

"Look, we been going about gettin' to the bag all wrong," I told my brother and Murph.

"How you figure that?" Murph asked.

"Yea, because if you ask me we been a'ight," Trip added.

We were sitting in my truck at the Circle K gas station on Hope Mills Road that basically sat inside my hood.

"Check this out," I pulled a .38 special snub nose out, and sat it in my lap. "This is our key to taking getting that bag to another level. This is the key to the city."

"I'm not understanding what you're trying to say," Trip said.

"Bra, we done selling work! We about to start robbing these niggas. Do y'all understand that that nigga took us for all we had in fifteen minutes? And how long did it take us to make that?" I asked them both.

"All week," Murph said.

"So now do you see my logic? Now, if y'all want to keep hustling, that's on y'all, but I'm on some other shit. So what it's gon' be?"

"Fuck it! Let's scrape these niggas," Murph said.

"I'm with it," Trip said hesitantly.

That was all I needed to hear. The city was in for a rude awakening. I reached under my seat and threw Murph and Trip each a ski mask.

"We about to hit a lick right now," I informed them.

"Who?" they both asked. "And where our pistol?"

"We gon' get y'all some hammers, but right now time is of the essence. And we about to hit DJ."

DJ was an older nigga in my hood; he stayed two streets over from my house. DJ was the weed man; he kept some gas,

19

but he always taxed us. Like Gucci Mane said, I *robbed the weed man cuz the nigga tried to tax me*.

" Fuck 'em," Murph said.

"That's a fact! I'm tired of that nigga anyway," Trip said.

That was all I needed to hear. As long as I had my niggas with me I felt like I was unstoppable! I pulled out and got on DJ's street. The closer we got to his house, the more upset my stomach got. I knew we were stepping into uncharted territory. At least for us.

One wrong step could lead us to an early grave. And the truth of the matter was that I didn't even have a plan! But three against one, I felt like we couldn't lose. I also knew his mom stayed there, so I was banking on DJ to just let us have it to keep his mom out of danger. We rode past DJ's house and saw DJ sitting in his red Cutlass with the doors open blasting some 21 Savage. When I saw this, I got my idea. I drove to the street over which was North Sumac, and parked.

"This is what we're going to do. While he in his car blasting that music, we gon' creep in through the back and wait for him to come in. Then it's game time."

We hopped out the truck and went through the yard behind DJ's.

We hopped the fence, and rushed up to his backdoor. I kicked the door in, and ran to the front of the house. I peeped out the window to make sure DJ was still in his car, but he was walking up to the front door, and he wasn't alone. He was coming towards the house with a short dark-skinned dude. Fuck!

"He coming, he coming!" I whispered harshly. "Masks!" I said when I saw Trip and Murph were still barefaced. I didn't plan on him knowing it was us that was robbing him, and I definitely wasn't planning on DJ to have company.

I stepped behind the front door, so that when it opened I would be behind them when they came in.

"I been waiting on your ass for two hours," DJ told the dude he was with, as they walked in, leaving the door open.

"I had to handle some other business," the dude said.

When they got all the way in the house, I stepped out behind them. "Don't fucking move!" I put the gun to the back of DJ's head.

"What the fuck is this?" the dark-skinned dude asked, looking at DJ.

"Shut up!" Murph rushed into the room with a Glock in his hand. Trip ran into the living room with his hand under his shirt, pointing as if he had a gun. It took me everything not to burst out laughing.

"Get on the floor and put your face in the carpet." I slapped DJ in the back of the head with the .38.

DJ laid flat on the floor, and his homeboy did the same.

"Where it at?" I asked.

"Face?" DJ said my name, turning to look back, earning him a kick to the face. We looked at each other, and I pulled my mask off. He knew it was me! Things couldn't have gotten any worse. I had never killed anybody before. I had never even shot anyone. But I knew DJ would blow smoke, and on top of that he knew where we stayed. And there was no way I was going to allow him to shoot my house up and risk the chance of a bullet hitting my mom. But I didn't know if I had it in me to kill him, though. All I wanted was to rob him and dip out. I wasn't trying to catch a body.

"Make this shit easy and tell me where everything's at?" I squatted down by DJ's head.

"Nigga, you set me up," DJ's man said to him.

"If you say one more thing, you better finish your sentence with a prayer because they'll be the last words you ever say," Murph told him.

"I ain't giving you lil' nigga shit! Don't y'all niggas know I know where your mother stay at?" DJ snapped, and tried to sit up.

Bah!Bah! The .38 in my hand jumped twice, leaving two holes in DJ's forehead. He died looking me in my eyes. I don't know what happened but something inside of me clicked. Seeing DJ's eyes gloss over as his life left his body gave me a feeling I had never felt before, and I *loved* it! I looked over to his man, and he must've seen it too because he instantly turned into a bitch.

"Please, man! Just let me go. I got sixty bands and thirty pounds of banana kush in my trunk under the spare tire." *Bah! Bah! Bah!* I gave him the last three rounds in the .38, and stood up. When I looked at Murph and Trip, they were staring at me with their mouths halfway open.

"What are y'all looking at? We don't know how much time we got before his mom pull up, search the house," I said, searching DJ and his man. I got a Heckler and Koch .45 off DJ, and ten racks. His homeboy only had three racks. I got his car keys out his pocket, and stood up. When I stood up, Trip and Murph were still looking at me slack jawed.

"Bro! You killed them," Trip said.

I didn't respond. I ran out the house, and popped the trunk to dude's car. The first thing I saw was a gold AK with two see-through banana clips. I slung it over my shoulder, moved the spare tire, and saw two book bags. I grabbed them, and ran back in the house. The minute I stepped back in the house, I heard Trip yell: "Found it!"

He came running out the back with a pillowcase in his hand.

"Let's go!" I yelled.

We ran, hopped the fence, got in my truck, and swerved off. We couldn't go to my house because my mom was nosey, and I wasn't going to risk her seeing the weed and money. She didn't know that me and Trip were in the streets like we were. To her, we were still her babies; I planned on keeping it that way. We went to Murph's house because he stayed in a split level with his mom and little brother. He had the whole bottom floor to himself. During the whole ride to his house, no one said a word; it was dead quiet. I guess the magnitude of what had just transpired was starting to sink in. We got to Murph's house, and went straight to Murph's room. I dumped the two book bags out, and Trip dumped the pillowcase out. We counted the money, and it came out to a hundred and twenty racks and forty-five pounds of some banana kush. We each got forty bands and fifteen pounds.

"Now that's what the fuck I'm talking about!" I screamed.

I had never had this much money for such a little bit of work.

"Fuck trapping, nigga. I'm jacking!" Murph thumbed through his cut of money.

"Yeah, I can't front—That shit was mad easy," added Trip.

"And this is only the beginning. Just wait and see." The wheels in my head were spinning.

Nicholas Lock

Chapter Three

"Angie, why you ain't cooked nothing to eat?" I asked. I was at her house, chilling. Angie stayed on the same street as me. She stayed on one corner of Redwood, and I stayed on the other. Angie was forty-one, and had no kids. She had a deep caramel complexion, and black bone straight hair that flowed downwards, brushing the handful of booty she had. Angie had naturally arched eyebrows, and lips that God made for kissing and sucking dick. Behind those lips were some of the straightest and whitest teeth I'd ever seen. She was petite and endowed with shapely titties. Angie worked at Cape Fear Valley Hospital as the lead nurse on the ICU floor. She was also a smoker. She wasn't an all-out crackhead, but she still smoked crack. I was trying to get her to quit because in my eyes she was too sexy to be smoking.

"Boy, I just got home, I ain't even washed my ass yet! And you not my man to be telling me when to cook!" She walked in the back, and I followed her.

"Whose fault is that?" I questioned.

"Whose fault is what?"

"The reason I'm not your man."

"Boy, bye! First off, you're jailbait and second off, I don't think Rai'chell would appreciate that too much." She took her top off, revealing a red Victoria Secret bra. I had seen Angie naked plenty of times, so it wasn't anything new to me. I had tried to give her an eight ball of hard to let me fuck, and she had cussed me out so bad that I ended up giving her the eight ball. We had fallen out for a couple of days, but we ended up getting back cool, and from that day forth we had a good level of understanding. But I still slid a slick comment in from time to time. I hated that she always brought up Rai'chell when I would say something fly. Angie was one of the few people

25

that knew how I felt about Rai'chell. Angie knew I had a real soft spot for Rai'chell, and would go to the ends of the earth to see her happy.

"Yeah, you need a bath, I smell you," I joked, taking a seat on her queen-size bed.

"Might be your upper lip." She threw her shirt at me, and walked into the bathroom.

While Angie went to take a shower, I called my nigga— Ross. He was supposed to be buying the fifteen pounds I had.

"What up, G?" I asked, when he answered.

"Not shit, trying to get this money as usual."

Ross was another one of my day one niggas; he was older than me by two years. Ross was the one that got me into hustling in the first place. He took hustling to a whole 'nother level.

"You still trying to get those?" I needed to know.

"Damn, I forgot! Where you at?"

"On Redwood at Angie's house."

"I'll be there in twenty," he said, and hung up.

I went and grabbed the fifteen pounds out of Angie's closet, and sat them on the bed. I knew twenty minutes for Ross meant he'd be here in an hour.

I was selling the pounds for twenty-five hundred a pop, so I was making a thirty-seven thousand dollar profit. Not bad for a few minutes of work. I was already plotting on who we were going to stick first. Now I understood what French Montana was rapping about when he said, stay scheming. There weren't too many times throughout the day where you would catch me not thinking about robbing. Angie came out the shower in a towel, and her hair up in a bun. I started to say something, but then I saw the glazed look her eyes got when she was high. I grabbed the weed up, and walked into the living room. I kicked my feet up on the coffee table, and turned the TV on.

"Get your feet off my table." Angie swiped my feet. "And what your hungry ass want to eat?"

"Spaghetti and garlic bread. And you work at the hospital, so what's good with this COVID-19 shit? Should I be worried or nah?" I asked because that was all the news was talking about. She spoke as she went to the kitchen, and I could still hear her voice while she was there.

"Honestly it's too early to say, but I do know it's more dangerous to elderly people and people who have pre-existing conditions, especially respiratory problems. And I see you in your feelings too."

"I'm good just so long as you cook." I propped my feet back on the table.

Beep! Beep! A car blew its horn outside. I looked out the window, and saw Ross's 1972 Chevelle SS on twenty-fours. He had recently got the Chevelle painted candy blue, with the black racing stripe down the middle. I stepped out the front door, as a bright green Camaro with white dollar signs etched all over it pulled up to the end of the driveway. The tint on the new Camaro prevented me from seeing who was inside. Before I could step off the porch, the windows of the Camaro rolled down, and all I saw were gun barrels.

"Ross, watch out!" I yelled, and dived back into the house as the shots started to ring out.

Tat! Tat! Tat! Tat! Tat! Tat!

"Aahh!" Angie yelled as the windows to the house shattered.

"Get down!" I scrambled to Angie, yanked her to the floor, and covered her with my body.

The shooting stopped, and I ran outside to check on my nigga. Ross's Chevelle was littered with bullet holes. I opened his door, and he fell out onto the ground.

"What happened?" Murph rode up in the new Crown Victoria he had just bought, with Trip riding shotgun.

"Niggas rode up and started busting," I said, picking Ross up and carrying him to Murph's car. It looked like Ross was bleeding from everywhere. I didn't know what to do.

"Keep your eyes open!" I yelled because Ross kept trying to close his eyes. "Hurry up, bra! And call Nicole and tell her what's up."

Nicole was Ross's older sister.

"Roll the windows up," Ross said, barely above a whisper. We rolled the windows up, and five minutes later Ross said, "Roll the windows down." We went through the window shit twice before we pulled into Cape Fear Valley. Me and Trip carried Ross into the emergency room where the nurses took him out of our hands, and rushed him into the back.

"Fuck!" I screamed, walking outside.

"Yo, who the fuck was it?" Murph was ready to ride.

I sighed before replying. "I didn't see their face. All I saw was the car they were riding in, and guns. It had to be some beef Ross had because they definitely weren't gunning for me. You can tell that by the amount of bullet holes Ross's whip took."

"What kind of car was it?" asked Trip.

"A bright green Camaro with dollar signs on it."

"Rude Boy and his brother Rampage. That's Rampage's car. They run 301. Ross told me about a month ago that they had ran down on him, talking about he couldn't hustle on 301, but you know bro won't trying to hear that." Trip put the pieces to the puzzle together.

"Where they be at on 301 and what they look like?" I questioned.

"Everywhere on 301, but I know they be in Taylors Creek a lot. Rude Boy is short, dark-skinned with six big ass dreads. He's the oldest at forty. He's the one that really runs the show. Rampage is our height at 6'0, dark-skinned, big nose, and he always got his hair in cornrows. Rampage is twenty-nine. He get money too but he's more inclined to be on his hot boy shit."

"Let's ride then," I said.

We left with one thing on our mind—Murder.

Nicholas Lock

Chapter Four

Okay, green light, uh, uh/Pistol in the party don't seem right/Lil' bro off that Molly can't think right/It's about to be a fuckin' green light/I get in my feelings off that Henn', dawg/I gon' be this way until the end, dawg/I got too much on my mind and I cannot get it off. Rod Wave's hit was blasting out the Alpine speakers of Murph's Crown Vic.

We were on our way to see about this Rude Boy character and his brother Rampage. Nobody had said anything since leaving Murph's house and picking up our guns. I had the gold AK-47 laying across my lap, and a chrome .9 beside me. Murph had twin Glock .30's, and Trip had a Sig .40. Every pistol in the car had extendos, so we had over two hundred shots to play with. Rude Boy and Rampage were in for a long night. I had already slumped DJ and his man, so I already knew what it was like to have blood on my hands. Tonight though, Trip and Murph were going to get theirs dirty. I couldn't get the image of Ross bleeding out of my mind. Somebody else was about to feel the same way I felt seeing my boy laid out like that.

"Yo, cut the music down real quick, this Nicole calling. What's good?"

"Ross is out of surgery, and he's good. The surgeon said one of his lungs had collapsed, and that if y'all wouldn't have gotten him to the hospital when you did, he would've suffocated. When he wakes up, they said he could go home but he has to be on bed rest for the next few weeks." Nicole told me the good news, which made me sigh with relief.

That was why Ross kept telling me to roll the windows up and down; he couldn't breathe. I could breathe easier, knowing my boy was out of the woods. He was going to be an

31

integral part of my plans. Since I wasn't trapping anymore, all the work I got I was going to sell to Ross for the low. It was going to be a win-win for both parties. I wanted to make sure all my day ones had a spot at the table.

"Good luck keeping him in bed for two weeks," I told Nicole.

"Face, don't do nothing crazy, it's not worth it," she tried giving me some advice.

"Would it have been worth it if Ross had gotten killed?" I questioned, and she got quiet. "You shoot my cat, I kill your dog."

"Be safe," was her reply.

"Always." I hung up.

We pulled into Taylors Creek, as the clouds moved, revealing a full moon. *A full moon could be looked upon as good luck or bad luck*, I thought, looking up into the night sky. Hopefully, it was going to be good luck on our behalf. Murph slowed the Vic down, and cruised through. Taylors Creek was nothing more than a big trailer park with a house here and there. And a majority of the trailers, whether they were single wide or double wide, had fences around them. We were going in blind because neither of us knew Rude Boy's exact location, but we did know the type of car they were in. Things worked out in our favor because we bent a corner, and there sat the green Camaro. There were about ten niggas milling about. I was looking for two in particular, though. I spotted Rude Boy first. He had done me a favor by being dressed in an all-white Adidas tracksuit. I didn't see Rampage, but I could care less. I was hell bent on seeing somebody bleed out. None of the dudes paid us any attention, as we cruised down the block towards them. I rolled my window down as we got closer. When we got within a few feet of Rude Boy, I came out the back window with the gold choppa.

Kah! Kah! Kah! Boc! Boc! Boc! Trip's Sig sounded off with my Choppa, causing niggas to break out. I was trying to take Rude Boy out the game, but he must've been a track star in high school because it seemed like he was dodging the .223 bullets from the AK the same way Barry Saunders used to dodge linebackers.

"Yea, nigga!" Trip said, as a nigga he was busting at fell face first into the ground and lay still. I sat on the windowsill, and let the Choppa talk. *Kah! Kah! Kah!* I was trying my damndest to put a hole in Rude Boy's back, yet I was hitting everything but him. Obviously, Murph was thinking the same thing I was because he hopped out the driver seat, and started shooting the twin Glocks he had while walking with the car! My nigga was putting on!

"Like that, nigga!" Murph dropped two dudes, and got back in to drive.

I ran out of bullets in the first clip, and ducked back in the car to grab the other one. It wasn't a chance in hell I was going to allow both of them to outdo me. I came back out the window, and that's when I saw Rampage smiling at me. He had a Draco pointed in my direction. I was able to bring the choppa up, as Rampage let the Draco spit. The first couple of bullets struck the AK, knocking it out of my hands and onto the street. The next few rounds hit the door, making Murph hit the gas, and making me the luckiest nigga in the world because Rampage had me dead to rights. We sped out of Taylors Creek with our mission only halfway accomplished. They shot Ross, and we killed three of their niggas, but the way Rampage had been smiling and shooting the Draco led me to believe we'd be crossing paths again in the near future. However, I planned on being the one smiling when that time arrives.

***

"Diqueena, mind your business! And why you always taking her side?" I asked my homegirl, who just so happened to be doing Rai'chell's hair.

"Because I'm right, and she was my friend first," Rai'chell said.

Diqueena had been cool with Rai'chell first, but I felt like me and her had a strong bond.

"Diqueena, who you love more?" I asked, stretching out across her couch.

"Boy, hush," Diqueena grinned, showing off her pearly white teeth.

If I hadn't met Rai'chell, I would have hollered at Diqueena's pretty ass. She had the prettiest dark skin and high cheekbones, giving her a regal look. Diqueena was short, too. She couldn't have been more than five feet, and she had the body of the singer Jhene Aiko. Then she had the most down-to-earth personality there was, making her much more appealing.

"And get your feet off my mama couch before she cuss you out. You know how Rai'chell is, so if you just stay out them hoes faces, she wouldn't be mad." Diqueena got on my case.

"Oh, I see what's going on." I stood up to leave.

"Where you going?" asked Rai'chell.

"Away from y'all. Y'all not about to double team me."

"No!" Rai'chell got up, and stood in front of the door. "You're not about to leave," she pouted.

"Ain't you staying here tonight?" I questioned, and she nodded by way of saying *yes*. "Okay then. I'll be back later on tonight." I grabbed her by the hips and leaned down to kiss her.

"You promise?" She got up on her toes to give me a kiss.

"Yeah, girl, now move." I left out Diqueena's house with plans on coming back because I had to have some of Rai'chell's love.

***

"Hand me my phone," Rai'chell whispered, trying to be quiet. It was one in the morning, and me and Rai'chell were laying in Diqueena's living room on a pallet on the floor. I handed her her phone, and she put Big Sean's song "Body Language" on, and cut the TV off.

"Face, I want your last name." She crawled back under the covers, and snuggled up against my chest.

"You can have it." I kissed her on the forehead, making her smile.

"You love me, boy?"

"More than you know." I rubbed on her butt.

"Let me see," Rai'chell kissed me on the lips, and started pushing my head down.

I sucked on her neck while undoing her bra. I sucked one of her nipples in my mouth, causing her to take in a quick breath. She pushed my head again, trying to get me to go lower. Rai'chell was shy and dinky as hell, so she wasn't going to outright tell me to eat her pussy. Her pushing the top of my head was her way of telling me to eat her love box. I got down between her legs, and could smell her sweet scent through the pink lace thong she was wearing.

"Oohh!" she moaned, grabbing the back of my head, as I bit on her clit through her thong.

I pulled the thong to the side, and ran my tongue over her sex lips, making Rai'chell lock her legs around my head. I sucked her clit into my mouth, making her forget where we were because she yelled my name.

"You better hush before Diqueena mama wake up."

"I can't help it, your tongue driving me crazy," she smiled.

"And that's why you're not getting any more of it." I climbed on top of her.

I pulled her thong off, and tossed it to the side. I was trying not to look her in the face because every time we got ready to fuck, she would have this look on her face that drove me crazy. It was really her eyes that did it. Her eyes would be closed to slits, and she would stare at me through the slits. I used my thumb to guide my pole into her gushy opening.

"You better go slow too," Rai'chell said, as I tried to slide into her.

"Damn boo," I said into her ear, as I got halfway in. Rai'chell's love tunnel was so wet and tight, I was having a hard time controlling myself.

"Baby, yesss," she moaned, wrapping her legs around my back. I started pulling all the way out, and slamming back into her. It wasn't too often that we fucked without a condom because she didn't want to have kids at the moment, so I had to enjoy the special occasion. I got up on my hands in the push up position, and began to drill her.

"Face! Face! Face!" she moaned out, putting her hand on my stomach. "Stop trying to be cute." Rai'chell got up on her elbows, and pushed me out of her.

"What's up?" I was trying to fuck, not talk.

"You can't do me like that," she whined. "You gon' get us caught."

" Come on then."

We put our clothes on, and went and got in the backseat of my truck. I didn't waste any time! I bent Rai'chell over, and dug her back out.

"I'm about to cum, Face!" she screamed.

"Me too," I said, speeding my strokes up.

Every time I would stroke her, she would try to raise up, but I had her by the waist so she was forced to take every inch I had. I released deep inside her.

"Ugh! You gon' have my coochie hurting tomorrow. You make me sick." She punched me playfully.

"You love me though," I boasted.

"Too much, nigga, so know if you ever play me to the left, I'm gon' fuck your world up!" Rai'chell pulled her jeans on, and sat in my lap.

"Yeah, that way."

I carried my baby back into the house, and laid with her until she fell asleep. Then I locked the door, and went home to get in my own bed. I needed some rest. We had a big football game the next day.

Nicholas Lock

Chapter Five

It was Friday night, and we had a big game versus the South View Tigers. We were undefeated, and trying to stay that way. Then the college Scouts were going to be there, and there was one in particular that we wanted to show out for the North Carolina Tar Heels. It would be nice to get a scholarship offer from my favorite team, but I'd be happier if Trip got one. Because, like I said before, I was thugging with no brakes, and Trip was NFL-ready. If he made it to the pro's, all would be well. He would be a multimillionaire, and I know he would make sure I was straight. Until then, it was jack or die for me.

"What the hell is y'alls problem?" Coach Puah yelled. We were down by seventeen at halftime, and Coach was livid.

"We got you, Coach. Defense! It's no excuse why they keep scoring on us! So for the next two quarters they don't get so much as a field goal!" I yelled. "Eagles on three. One, two, three! Eagles!"

We ran out the locker room, and onto the field. I looked up into the stands trying to see if I could spot the scouts, and saw Rude Boy and Rampage! What they were doing at a high school football game was beyond me, but I was going to keep my helmet on so Rampage wouldn't recognize me. He was the only one that actually looked me in the face that night; everybody else had been focused on running.

"Trip, Murph!" I called them over.

"What's good?" Trip walked over to where I was.

"Look in the stands at the row behind the band," I told him, looking the opposite way.

"Oh shit!" Murph said.

"And they're pointing at us," Trip added.

I turned to see Rampage pointing us out to Rude Boy and a heavyset dark-skinned man with a temp fade. I locked eyes with Rude Boy and Rampage, and they all nodded. I wasn't too concerned at the moment because we were on school grounds, and there were a ton of police around. Besides, I knew they weren't anywhere near as retarded as me. Slumping DJ had turned me into a savage. I would get to letting my hammer talk at the slightest provocation; but, to be on the safe side, I called Rai'chell over to me. She came to all our games.

"Call Ross and tell him Rude Boy and Rampage are up here at the game and we down bad."

She pulled her phone out and called Ross. Ross wasn't home two days before he was back in the streets, trapping. It was going to take more than a few bullet wounds to keep Ross from getting to the bag. He ate, slept and shitted trapping. Since getting shot, Ross hustled on 301 without any regards for anybody or anything. And he was sending shells Rude Boy and Rampage's way every chance he got. So I knew by telling Ross they were at the game, they were going to have their hands full the minute he spotted them.

"He on the way," Rai'chell said. "You need me to do anything else?" Rai'chell wanted to be gangsta so bad it was funny.

"Nah, just stay pretty."

I had to get my head back in the game so I could focus. We were starting the second half on defense, so me and Murph were up. South View had one of the best—if not the best—running back in North Carolina. He had already committed to play for Alabama. They lined up on their twenty yard line, and handed the ball to their running back— Zyaire. He tried to hit an A-gap, but I was already there waiting for him. *Crack!* Our helmets collided, sounding like a gunshot. He fell a yard behind the line of scrimmage.

"Let's go!" I screamed, slapping my helmet.

They lined up, and tried to run another running play, but this time Murph was in the backfield before Zyaire could get the ball. The quarterback tried to pull the ball back, but Murph hit him, forcing the ball out of his hands. One of my teammates jumped on the ball; we were back in the game! Trip and the offense got on the field, and scored a touchdown on Trip's first pass.

"That's how you do that!" Murph yelled, slapping Trip on the back, as he came off the field.

I looked up in the stands: Rude Boy and his cronies were gone. I put them out of my mind, and focused on putting the game away. In the end, when all was said and done, Douglas Byrd came out on top. We beat them by ten, keeping our undefeated season alive. As we walked to our bus, I saw Ross sitting on the hood of his Cadillac. Rude Boy was nowhere to be seen, which was a good thing for him. Me and Ross acknowledged each other with a nod, and I got on the bus. I needed to find out what Rude Boy had going on.

***

"That's his Hummer right there," Ross pointed to a yellow H2 sitting on 30's in a Bojangles parking lot.

I made a U-turn, and grabbed my gun off my lap. We had gotten lucky with this one. Me and Ross were really just chilling, smoking, and riding around the city while I filled him in on the plan. I had as far as him selling all the work I hit niggas for. In the process of us getting everything together, he spotted Rude Boy's Hummer. Good for us, bad for him. I pulled off Skibo Road, and parked behind the H2 so he couldn't back out. We were about to send Rude Boy to the afterlife the minute he walked out of Bojangles. Ross rolled his window down, and cocked the Russian AK-47 he had between his legs. I knew he wanted Rude Boy bad. After waiting ten minutes, I said *fuck it,* and got out. I was always the one quickest to fight, but now that I had started playing with the fiyah, I was real quick to let that bitch go!

Ross got out, and leaned up against the truck with his door open. For easy access to the choppa, I pulled my hood over my head and walked in the fast food chicken spot. At first glance I didn't see him, so I checked the bathroom; there was still no trace of Rude Boy. I went back outside to let my nigga know he was tripping, when a voice behind me said, "Who the fuck is blocking me in?"

I turned to see what could only be described as an angel. She stood about 5'7, with green eyes, and had the smoothest peanut butter brown skin I had ever seen. I was trying to find a flaw, but didn't see one. She was perfect in every sense; even her toes were exquisite, as they played peek-a-boo in the Jimmy Choo heels she was wearing. Her silky black hair was real kinky, with burgundy highlights that hung to her waist. Her dress game was on point. The white Roberto Cavalli pantsuit she wore gave her a classy look, and put emphasis on her hourglass shape. She had a shape like that of Megan thee Stallion, and all the diamonds she had on let me know she was either on her shit or she had a nigga spoiling her—or a little bit of both.

"Um—Hello!" She waved her hand in front of my face, sounding real proper.

"What up, Angel?"

"*Angel*? You have me mistaken. My name is Cynthia, and is this your truck?"

"Well, it should be, Angel. God took his time when he was making you. I've been trying to find a flaw but I can't." My compliment made her blush.

"Thank you but I have a boyfriend."

"Are you happy though?" I looked her up and down.

"Excuse me?"

I walked up on her until we were face to face.

"I asked, *are you happy*? Are you in love?" I stared in her green eyes.

She paused before saying, "That's none of your business, and move your truck before I call him."

I laughed hard as hell.

"Please call him, please. And you're not answering my question. Give me my answer so let me make you happy." I laid it on thick.

It was really in her best interest to give a nigga some play, but not because I couldn't take rejection; more so because she was too beautiful to be getting hurt. But her being Rude Boy's lady put her in a bad position. She was about to be snatched up and put in the trunk.

"How can you make me happy?" she smirked, putting her hand on her hip.

"By treating you like the angel you are, and making sure all your needs are met—whether they're physical, mental or emotional." I wiped the smirk off her face.

She shrugged and said, "It's your funeral. Let me see your phone so you can move your truck and I can go." I got her number, got in the truck, and pulled off. I was going to fuck a bad bitch, and set Rude Boy up all in one motion.

Nicholas Lock

Chapter Six

I don't know how it happened. Well, I do know how it happened. We were on our BMF shit—*Blowing money fast!* We ran through the money from the lick like it was water. Part of it was due to the fact that we'd never had that much money at one time, plus we were young. We did have a little to show for it, depending on who you asked and how you looked at it. Of course, we got dumb fresh and got our jewelry game up, but we had snapped out in the car department.

Murph had his Crown Vic painted outrageous red, and airbrushed on the sides. *Big Red* was one of the nicknames Murph went by. The interior was white and red, with *Big Red* stitched into the headrests. The seats were all white with red stitching. Murph already had a system, but he put a TV in the dashboard, and in the back of both headrests. He topped it off with some red and white 26's. Trip surprised us because, instead of being his usual frugal self, he went and got a baby blue S550. The only thing Trip did to it was, put some tint on the windows, and some 22's on the tires.

Me, I went and bought the new Charger. I had the bottom painted white, and the top half black. I had the scene where Scarface (in the 1983 remake of the 1932 Paul Muni film of the same name) was shooting the M16 airbrushed on the sides, and on the hood the scene where Scarface was sitting behind his desk with a Beretta next to his enormous pile of cocaine during the climatic ending of the film. The paint job alone had set me back twelve racks. The interior was all black, with white stitching. I put TVs in the headrests and some 28's. But what made the Charger stand out was that the roof was all glass! I had a button to block me from view by a sliding curtain.

All that was the reason we were in a stolen Malibu in Meadowwood, watching Jason's trap, listening to Freddie Gibbs' "Rob Me A Nigga". I had been on Jason for the last two weeks, trying to find out how best to get at him. Jason was an older dude, probably around forty or so, and he had been hustling rocks forever and a day. There wasn't a doubt in my mind whether or not he was caked up. He was one of those lucky niggas that had never been locked up or suffered any major setbacks. To my knowledge, he'd never been robbed either, so I knew he was sitting real good. Then he popped out with the new Aston Martin Vanquish. That solidified the bad night he was about to have.

"What we waiting on?" Murph asked, ready to click.

"Her," I said, as a grey Maserati Ghibli pulled up outside the trap.

Every other night Jason's girlfriend brought him something to eat, and tonight was no different. I pulled my mask down, and cocked the .10 mm I had, then Murph and Trap followed suit. When Jason's girlfriend went outside my line of vision in the house, I got out and approached the Maserati. While watching Jason's trap, I noticed his girl never locked the doors. I eased up to the car, opened the door behind the driver and got in. I initially planned on running in the trap, but he'd been in the game a long time so I was sure Jason wasn't dumb enough to have a meal ticket in the trap. But I could almost guarantee his house was strapped. I was going to make Jason's girl take me to their house while Trip and Murph followed behind us. I switched off the interior light so that it wouldn't come on when she opened the door. After about ten minutes, she came back out but Jason was with her. This was going to fuck shit up! If they saw me, I was upping the .10mm and putting it to use. I just hoped the girl knew where the money was. She opened the car door and stuck one of her legs inside, keeping the other one on the driveway as she faced Jason.

"What time you coming home, baby?" she asked Jason.

"Don't start, Lisa, we already went over this," he sighed.

"Whatever, Jason!" She huffed and slammed the car door. "I hate that nigga!" she said to herself, pounding on the steering wheel, as she sped out of the neighborhood.

"That means you don't have a problem giving me all his shit then." I put the gun to her head.

"Aahh!" She slammed on brakes.

"Unless you plan on dying, I suggest you keep driving."

"Please don't hurt me," she pleaded, driving off.

"All you have to do is, take me to your house and you'll live. If you try something stupid, you won't live to see the sunrise."

She nodded as if she understood. She drove us from Strickland Bridge Road to Hope Mills, a city on the outside of Fayetteville. Everything about it screamed money, from the perfectly manicured yards with the ivory statues to the wraparound driveways with the luxury cars. *Jason had done well for himself,* I thought, as we pulled into a two-story house. She hit the garage door opener, drove into the garage, and cut the car off.

"Now what?" she asked.

"Don't play with me. You know what this shit hitting for. We about to go in here and you're going to tell me where everything is at. Or you can play games, get killed and I'll wait for Jason and still get what I came for. The choice is yours."

After considering the ultimatum I gave her, she said: "My jewelry and shit stays. I don't give a fuck about his."

I laughed. "You know what, shawty? You got that, now come on."

We got out of the car with me thinking bitches ain't shit. Trip and Murph rushed into the garage, and closed the garage door. She quickly opened the door, letting us into the house.

"Where the money?" Murph grabbed her by the back of the neck.

"Nigga, you better get your hands off me!" She tried to snatch away from Murph, but his grip was too tight. Shorty was either crazy or she was with the shits because after the initial shock of me being in her backseat, she was trying to get jazzy.

"Bitch, you better calm down!" Murph snapped.

"Lisa, just tell us where it's at," I said.

"If you tell this light-skinned ass nigga to let my neck go, then I'll show you."

Murph looked at me, and I nodded. He let her go, and she mean-mugged him. *Pow!* Murph slapped her with the butt of his .45, dropping her to her knees.

I scowled at her. "My patience is wearing thin. Remember what I told you about letting you live. Well, you need to do your part." She stood up on wobbly legs, and walked us to the master bedroom.

"The safe is in the closet behind the clothes—The combo is 4, 13, 8, 13," she said, and plopped down on the bed, rubbing the knot on her forehead.

Trip, who had been silent for the whole ordeal, checked the safe. He looked back after opening it, and smiled. I walked over to the closet, and whistled. There were stacks and stacks of money in the safe, but something didn't seem right. I turned to look at Jason's girl and she was watching us with a smug expression.

"How much money is that?" I questioned.

"A hundred and twenty thousand," she answered drily.

Boom! I shot her in the leg, making her crumple to the floor.

"Where the real bread at?" I stood over her.

Jason had been hustling for too long to only have a hundred and twenty racks put up. And I was betting on it that she knew where he kept it.

"In the closet under the rug!" she yelled, holding her leg." Call me an ambulance!"

I ignored her, and watched Trip tear up the rug in the closet.

"Oh shit!" Trip yelled, and started throwing bundles of money wrapped in plastic at us.

I walked and looked over Trip's shoulder, and saw that under the rug was what looked to be safety deposit boxes lining the closet floor. The shit was major!

"Nigga, help!" Trip yelled at us.

Me and Murph started helping him take the money out. It took us ten minutes to get all the money out.

"How much money is this?" I asked the second time.

"Four point five." She glared at me.

"Four point five what?" asked Murph.

"Million," she said.

Boom! I blew the side of her face off. I was going downstairs, before her body hit the ground. I got some black trash bags, and rushed back upstairs. I wasn't even eighteen yet, and I was a millionaire! We threw the money in the bags, and walked out the house only to find two gun barrels aimed at us.

Nicholas Lock

Chapter Seven

We walked out the door, and into the arms of Fayetteville's finest—The Police!

"On the ground! Now!" they ordered.

They were too close for us to run past them, but images of the dead body flashed through my mind, and I turned and ran back through the house. I had to at least get the hammer off of me. Trip and Murph took off behind me. *Boom! Boom!* They started shooting at us! I ducked low, and kept running. I burst through the back door, and got clotheslined. I ended up on my back, looking up at a black dude in street clothes pointing his gun at Trip and Murph.

"Move and I'll kill you where you stand," he said calmly. The two policemen who we were running from caught up, and threw them on the ground. One was a short black dude with a bald head, and the other one was a tall, slim white dude with red hair and a full red beard. The black dude then pointed his gun at me, and said: "Today is your lucky day."

He patted me down, got my fiyah, and put me in some flex cuffs. I started doing the math in my head. I was seventeen, so if I got twenty years I'd be thirty-seven when I got out. They moved us into the living room, and put us on the floor, while the black dude in street clothes who I assumed was their superior went upstairs.

"Uunn! Man! You boys were gonna come off real good on this sting," the white dude said, opening one of the trash bags.

"Damn!" the black one said, seeing all the money.

"Lisa's dead," he said, coming back downstairs with his gun in hand.

Both policemen drew their guns, and pointed them our way when they heard him.

"Do y'all boys know that woman y'all executed was a police officer?" he asked.

I was done for! *I was going to be lucky not to get the death penalty*, I thought to myself.

"Of course you didn't. Now you have about five minutes to decide if you want to go to death row or do you want to walk out that door a free man." He sat down on the couch in front of us.

Trip and Murph both said they wanted option number two. I didn't say anything. My mind was trying to see through all the smoke. Certain things were starting to stick out. Where the fuck was their backup? They didn't even have radios! What the hell was going on? And why did he just ask us that loaded question. Of course, we wanted to walk out the house free but at what cost? I definitely wasn't gon' be no rat. He could kill that idea if that was the case.

"What's it going to be?" He looked at me.

"What is it gon' cost to walk out that door?" I wanted to know.

He smiled, showing he had two gold teeth in his mouth. "You're not just going to walk through the door without knowing what was on the other side. We might have us a new business partner. I was starting to get tired of Jason, anyway. You see, Jason works for us. Well, I wouldn't say *works for us,* but he pays us a monthly fee to keep him out of jail and protected from Jackboys like you guys. I saw you scoping Jason out three days ago, but I didn't take your young ass for a threat; that was my mistake. I'm Detective Corrigan, the black guy is Officer Wilkins, and Red Beard's name is Bernstein. Now you boys get out of here. I'll be in touch."

Trip and Murph didn't have to be told twice. They took off out the door. Hell no! Not me! I had 4.5 million reasons to stick around.

"What about the money and my gun?" I looked at the trash bags.

"That's ours, and I'll give you your gun back the next time we meet, now go!"

I reluctantly walked out. I had become a millionaire, and lost it all in one night, then him keeping my gun didn't sit right with me but I didn't have no wins.

***

"Baby, what's wrong?" Rai'chell asked me.

We were at my house, laying across the bed. I was still drunk about losing all that money, then the next day Jason and his girl were found dead. I knew who had killed Lisa, but Jason was a mystery to me, and I had an idea who had done it.

"Just thinking."

"About what?" She crawled on top of me, so we were face to face.

"Nosey ass." I kissed her on the nose, and palmed her butt. She was looking sexy as hell in her Chanel jeans and top. Rai'chell was a Chanel whore, she loved Chanel. Anytime we got into an argument, all I had to do is buy her something from the Chanel store, and all would be well.

I wasn't about to tell her I had gotten robbed by the police for four million cash, even though I knew she would believe me. I kept her in the dark for the most part about my illegal activities, even though she tried her damndest to get involved.

"Y'all want something from the store?" My mom stuck her head in my room. "Get off that girl." She ignored the fact that Rai'chell was on top of me.

"No, ma." I pushed Rai'chell off me, and sat up. "You ever heard of knocking?"

"In my house? I don't think so," my mom said, straightening one of my trophies up on my dresser. "Now when you get your own house I'll knock.

My mom was a short, feisty, caramel-colored lady with a razor-sharp tongue. She wore her hair in a bob similar to the one Halle Berry was known for. She looked ten years younger than her thirty-five years. People always thought she was our sister instead of our mother.

"They might need some condoms, ma." Trip looked over her shoulder.

"Shut up, boy!" my mom said.

Rai'chell turned bright red, bringing a smile to my face.

"Girl, I don't know why you blushing. I know you and my nasty son be having sex." This additional statement from my mom made Rai'chell turn a brighter shade of red.

"Ain't you going to the store, ma?" I had to save my baby.

"I'll be back later on," my mom said, leaving.

"I got something for you, Trip." Rai'chell pulled her iPhone out, and started typing.

I leaned over to see who she was texting, and saw it was Carmen—Trip's wifey. They'd been together since the sixth grade, and he loved her to death. I didn't even know Carmen and Rai'chell knew each other.

"See how much you be laughing in the next few minutes," she smirked.

"You ain't talking about shit," Trip said, as his phone rang.

"What up, boo?" he answered.

This is about to be good, I thought. I didn't know exactly what Rai'chell had told Carmen, but I was about to find out.

"Hell no!" Trip cut his eyes at Rai'chell. "Bae, don't act like that, a'ight." He hung up.

"I don't see you laughing now, nigga," Rai'chell teased.

"You need to get your girl, bra. She fucking my relationship up with Carmen. She told her I tried to fuck Bianca."

I bursted out laughing. Bianca was one of Rai'Chell's homegirls.

"Carmen talking about since I'm getting some from everywhere else, I won't be getting no more pussy from her," he whined.

"I'm sorry to hear that! Sucks to be you. Can you close my door on your way out because I'm about to get something you ain't."

Trip slammed my door, and I got up and locked it. I had to get me a quickie in before my mama got back.

Nicholas Lock

Chapter Eight

I had been kinda spooked by the wanna-be gangster/cop and his flunkies. They hadn't got up with me, and they didn't have my info; so, fuck 'em. *Jack or Die* was the motto, so I had a standard to uphold. They had taught me a valuable lesson, though. These niggas ain't living right, so I had to be extra careful with who I ran down on.

I still couldn't believe I had been a millionaire a few days ago, even if I hadn't been able to spend none of it. One thing was for certain, though: I wasn't going to just take it as no loss. I was going to get that money back. They were police-men, so I was going to get their addresses and get my money back!

Me and Trip were in my Charger, riding down Raeford Road, listening to "Said Something" by Moneybagg Yo, when I saw Cynthia walking inside the bowling alley. I pulled in the bowling alley, and got out.

"Damn, I'm tripping," I said, turning around.

"Man, what the hell you got going on?" my twin asked.

"I just saw Rude Boy's girl," I said, tucking my pistol.

Trip got out, thinking I was about to get it cracking, but I seriously doubted Rude Boy was with her. I had grabbed my gun just in case. Ross had been keeping it so hot on Rude Boy that he was keeping a low profile. Rampage himself was giv-ing as much as he got. Ross would shoot their trap up, and—not even fifteen minutes later—Rampage would return the fa-vor. No one had gotten killed recently, but that could change at any moment. At the moment, I really wasn't on my wild, wild west shit. I was trying to see what was up with Cynthia's sexy ass.

The bowling alley was jam-packed! It was hoes every-where. I had never seen the shit jumping like this. I was glad

I had my drips all the way up. I had on a brown Louis Vuitton button up, some tan slacks by Louis Vuitton, a brown Louis Vuitton belt, and a pair of brown and tan Louis Vuitton sneakers. I even had the brown and tan Louis V beanie covering my head. The only jewelry I had on was a gold rosary and a plain Jane Rolex. Trip had on some black Parish Nation straight legs, black Parish Nation sweater, a white Gucci belt, and some white Gucci sneakers. I spotted Cynthia at the far end of the room, and sat down, causing them to look at me like I was crazy. It was four of them, including Cynthia, and all of them were bad. One was Asian, and the other two were Hispanic, but I was focused on Cynthia. Recognition set in when she got a good look at my face, but then Trip came and sat down, causing her to pause. With us being identical, it was nearly impossible to tell us apart unless you really studied us. Even then the only difference between us was the scar on my face under my eye, but you had to be close up on me to see it. Cynthia looked from both of us, then asked me:

"Why didn't you call me?"

"I was scared of your boyfriend," Trip said the perfect reply, and I hadn't even told him about me and her conversation.

"Are you going to introduce me to your brother?" she asked, with her green eyes still staring at me.

"How do you know I'm the one you met?" I asked, smiling.

She walked over to me, and rubbed the scar under my eye. I grabbed her hand before she could snatch it away and pulled her down so that she was straddling me. She was being overly friendly all of a sudden, so I had to see how far she was going to go.

"A'ight boy!" She tried to get up, but I held her by her wide hips.

"This where you belong, in the lap of a King." I looked down at the camel toe poking out between the legs of the purple tights she was wearing.

"Who are these cuties?" the Asian chick asked.

Trip brought a smile to her face when he said: "I'm Trip, who he is doesn't matter right now. What's important is me and you getting to know each other."

"I'm Anika," she told Trip.

"Y'all don't have any friends for us?" the two Hispanic girls asked.

"I got you." I called Murph, and he just so happened to be with another one of our homeboys from the hood who was also our connect on guns. Tyrone was the guy's name. "They're on their way"

"Am I supposed to sit in your lap all night?" Cynthia looked me in the eyes.

"You got something else in mind?"

"Yea, come on!" Cynthia pulled me out onto the bowling lanes.

"Have you ever played before?" she asked.

"Yeah." I grabbed one of the bowling balls, and rolled it down the lane. It rolled right into the gutter.

"You suck," she laughed.

"I never said I was a professional but I bet I could beat you though," I boasted.

"What would you bet?" Her green eyes sparkled, thinking she had her a sucker.

"Make it light on yourself," I said nonchalantly.

"If I win you have to buy me the new Mercedes Coupé," Cynthia said with a straight face.

I looked at her like she was crazy.

"He might have bit off more than he can chew," one of her Hispanic homegirls said, smirking.

"Not with all that designer on," the other Hispanic chick said.

"I know for a fact that beanie alone cost four hundred and fifty dollars. I just saw it on the Louis Vuitton website."

"What do I get if I win?"

"Whatever you want," Cynthia said confidently.

"Remember you did this to yourself." I walked up, and whispered in her ear what I wanted, causing her to about choke on her Pepsi.

"Okay, bet!" She strutted off to grab her bowling ball, and reset the game.

What she didn't know was that she had fallen for the oldest trick in the book. I rolled that gutter ball on purpose. I was going to be a gentleman and allow her to win, until she made the comment about the Mercedes. Cynthia bowled on the regular because she had a customized bowling ball that was pink and white with her name on it. She went inside a bag, and came out with some pink and white bowling shoes.

"Bra, are you sure about this? It don't look like she no rookie." Trip walked over to me. "And what do you get if you win?"

"I get her for the whole weekend. She has to cater to my every need, and she's not allowed to wear anything but some six-inch stilettos. Now if you'll excuse me, I got some TLC to win." I smiled, then said to Cynthia: "Ladies first."

Cynthia went right to the lane, and bowled a strike. She high-fived her girls, and said: "Beat that."

Murph and Tyrone walked up, as I bowled a strike of my own. I nodded at the two Spanish broads, and they went in on them. While Murph and Tyrone started spitting their game, Cynthia bowled another strike. "You set me up!" she said, pushing me, and I pulled her to me.

"Maybe," I grinned. "Tap out now and I'll settle for only one day of you being my sex slave." I licked her on the neck.

"I don't quit." She strutted away, and rolled another strike. We went back and forth until she rolled and left three pins standing.

"It's over now," I set up to roll my ball, and she pushed me, sending my ball into the gutter.

"Ha-ha!" She leapt in the air.

I hurried up, and grabbed her bowling ball before she could react, and rolled a spare, wiping the smile off her face.

"Two weeks from now I'll be ready to collect," I said, and she rolled her eyes, and mumbled. "Whatever."

We chilled with them the rest of the night. In the process I learned that Cynthia and Rude Boy had broken up. She said she was tired of having to deal with him and his baby mama drama. This was just what I needed. Now I was going to sex her real good and get her to set him up. Murph, Tyrone and Trip got the numbers at the end of the night, and we made plans to get together again in about a week.

Nicholas Lock

Chapter Nine

I was having the worst week of my seventeen-year-old life! I was getting hit with bad break after bad break. First, somebody robbed Timbo; he was on my hit list. He was going to be our next lick. I had everything mapped out, then I heard from the streets that someone robbed him and shot him in the ass. It was being whispered that he'd got hit for four bricks and a hundred racks! So that was going to leave us assed out for a little bit longer. I only had twenty dollars left to my name! Something had to shake. Then I had got kicked out of school because of Kameesha's stupid ass. She was of the misconception that since we fucked that I was going to leave Rai'chell and be with her. So when I told her that won't happen, she made a scene which caught the attention of Mrs. Warner: the principal. She asked what the problem was, and Kameesha gave Mrs. Warner her phone. I had no clue as to what was going on until she asked Kameesha, "Who made this?" and Kameesha pointed at me.

"Come on, Mr. Lowe."

I cut my eyes at Kameesha before following Mrs. Warner to her office.

"This type of behavior will not be tolerated at my school!" she yelled.

"What are you talking about?" I was utterly lost.

She slid Kameesha's phone across the desk, and my eyes got big. The sound was off, but the video of Kameesha getting a train ran on her was playing. I looked at Mrs. Warner, and her white ass was so red that I laughed.

"So this is funny to you!?" she screamed. "You are hereby suspended for the rest of the year. Your mother will be informed of when you can come take your exams."

"What! I need to finish the season," I pleaded.

"You can either take your suspension, or I can suspend the entire football team. Your choice." She folded her arms across her chest.

I knew this was her way of getting me back for the years of hell I had been causing since my freshman year. I had to take one for the team. There was no way I could let Trip go down with me, especially since he had just got a full ride to North Carolina.

"Fuck you and this school!" I walked out her office, and ran into Rai'chell.

"You coming with me, Chell?" I asked.

"So you did fuck her?" Rai'chell scrunched her face up.

"Huh? That's the first thing you ask me?"

"Hell yes! You got me walking around here looking stupid!" She mushed me in my head. "I don't know why I stay with your dirty dick ass," she continued.

"I'm not in the mood for this dumb shit and since you don't know why you stay with me, then don't." I was already upset, and she was adding to it.

"You know what, Nymel? Fuck you! I'm through" Tears welled up in her eyes.

I walked away from her and our relationship. That wasn't the worst of it. I got home that night, and my mom kicked me out so I was staying at Angie's house.

"Why you got your face all balled up?" Angie asked me, as I sat in her living room, watching ESPN.

"Why do you smoke crack?" I said before I realized it.

Angie snapped her head back like she had been slapped, and walked to her room. I hadn't meant to snap on her, but I had a lot going on. I was frustrated. I don't care what nobody said, being broke fucked your mental up. I didn't understand how someone went through life broke. It was nothing like being able to go into a store and buy what you wanted. At the moment, I couldn't do that, and it was making me feel like a lame. I got up, and walked into the back. I had to apologize to Angie. She didn't deserve that; she had been nothing but good to me. I peeked in her room, and saw her under the covers, balled up in the fetal position.

"Angie," I called her name, and she ignored me.

I walked in and laid down beside her. I pulled the covers back, and saw she was crying.

"I'm sorry, Angie. I didn't mean to snap on you like that. I just got a lot on my mind right now."

"Face, do you think I like smoking crack? I've tried to quit but I can't." She wiped the tears from her eyes. I've been smoking it since college."

"College? How did you start?" I really wanted to know.

"I got tricked! To make a long story short, I was attending college in Greensboro at North Carolina A&T, and I liked to smoke weed. Well, the guy I was dealing with at the time said he had a Judy Fly, and pulled out a blunt. Me being green and naïve, I didn't think nothing of the fact that the blunt was already rolled. I thought a Judie Fly was a kind of weed. I hit it, and it took me to new heights. I had never been that high before in my life. I was higher than a giraffe."

I couldn't help but laugh. "Didn't you smell it?"

"Yeah, but like I told you, I was green to the streets and drugs, so I thought it was the weed that smelled like that. A few days later I asked him if he had some more, and he came over to my dorm but this time he rolled it in front of me. I asked him what were the tan rocks he was breaking up into the weed, and he said *crack* like it was no big deal. Now, I knew about crackheads but I don't know. He saw me hesitate, and told me it was the same thing we smoked the last time, and my pussy got wet. After a month of that, he introduced me to the stem and I've been doing it ever since. I've tried to quit but I can't shake it." She sobbed.

I wrapped my arms around her, as she cried. I felt bad for her.

"I got you, Angie, we gon' get you sober and keep you there." I kissed her on the forehead.

"You promise?" She looked at me with tears coating her eyelashes.

"Yeah," I said, and she kissed me. "What is you—" I started to ask, and she put her fingers to my lips.

I lay back as she came from under the covers and straddled me. Angie pulled her t-shirt over her head, freeing her little titties. They were only a mouthful, but her nipples had to be two inches long. She leaned up and put one in my mouth. I sucked her nipple in my mouth, and rolled my tongue around it, making her moan out.

"Mmmm." Angie leaned back, taking her nipple out my mouth. She grabbed my wife-beater and pulled it over my head. I knew where this was going! I wanted to ask her if she was sure, but I had been wanting to fuck her red ass for so long that I didn't want to risk her saying no. Don't judge me!

Angie sucked on my neck while massaging my dick through the Akoo jogging pants I was wearing. She kissed her way down my stomach, sending chills throughout my body. I kicked off the Nikes I had on, and Angie worked my jogging pants down my ankles, leaving me in my boxers. She still had on her balling shorts, but at the moment I wasn't complaining. Angie pulled my dick out and kissed the head. Her soft pink lips felt like heaven. She licked the precum that was sitting in the slit, slid my piece to the back of her throat, and let it come out her mouth with a soft pop.

"Quit playing, Angie." I tried to guide my head back down, but she moved my hand.

Angie put the head in her mouth, and looked up at me with her bedroom eyes, while going down inch by inch.

"Damn, Angie," I said, running my hand through her hair. This old cougar was blowing my mind.

I reached up, and pulled her gym shorts over her ass. She didn't have on any underwear. I rubbed on her ass with one hand, and used my other one to control her head. Angie grabbed the hand that was rubbing her ass, and moved it between her legs.

"Do it like this," she whispered, showing me how she liked to be touched. I had never had a woman show me how to please her; the shit was making my dick harder. I pulled her shorts all the way off, and lifted her onto my face, putting us in the sixty-nine.

"Oohh!" she moaned out the minute my tongue touched her clit. I had to show her I wasn't a rookie. I grabbed her hips so she couldn't run, and went in.

"Shit! Shit! Shit!" Angie yelled, as my mouth continued its assault on her love box.

I pushed her head back down onto my pole, and ran my tongue over her booty hole.

"Mmmm," she moaned around my manhood.

We got into a rhythm where the faster my tongue flicked her clit the faster she sucked my pole. Angie was doing something with her mouth that had me feeling like she was sucking my soul out. I had never had no head this good!

"I'm about to nut!"

"Wait for me!" she said.

I emptied my nut into her mouth the same time she drenched my face with her love potion. We curled up in the spoon position, and fell asleep sexually satisfied.

Nicholas Lock

Chapter Ten

The next few days, me and Angie were cooped up in the house, smoking loud and fucking like rabbits. Every time I looked at her, my dick got hard. We had just got done having a marathon sex session when she asked "What are we doing, Nymel?"

I knew something was coming, by the way she used my real name.

"Having fun." I had my eyes closed, dozing off.

"I don't have casual sex. I only give my loving to someone I care about and someone I'm with." She laid her head on my closet.

"Oh, you care about me?" I joked, and she reached down and grabbed my nuts.

"Don't play with me, boy" Angie squeezed.

"A'ight! A'ight!" My eyes snapped open.

"You know you my boyfriend, right?" She massaged my balls.

"Are you asking or telling me?"

"Both."

I thought about what she was saying. It wasn't like she was ugly. Angie was bad, but she smoked crack. Well, she used to.

"On one condition." I tilted her chin up so we were looking each other in the eyes. "You can't be smoking, bae, I can't be with you and you doing that."

"I haven't even thought about smoking these last few days, if you haven't noticed."

"Of course I noticed." I kissed her on her forehead and both her eyes, making her smile.

"So you a jackboy now?"

"Huh? Where you get that from?"

"Face, I'm not stupid. Y'all stopped hustling, but y'all still be having money out the ass." Angie let me know that her days of being green and naïve were long gone.

I was going to have to remind myself that Angie was forty-one, so she had seen it all. Her comment reminded me that all I had was a few dollars in my pockets.

"It's nothing for you to worry about though," I reassured her.

"Just be careful," she said, and closed her eyes.

While she dozed off, I laid there trying to think of a come up. This was the only thing about robbing that I hated. The times where I didn't have a lick lined up. When I was hustling, there was always money coming in. I had an emergency stash but it was really for just that—emergencies. Whether it be bail money or lawyer money, but me not having any walk-around-with money didn't account for an emergency. I could always stick one of the small-time D-boys, but that was too petty. I wanted big bucks. If I was going to risk it, then it had to be worth it, and a few racks weren't worth it. I had four potential victims, but I hadn't had time to scope them out, and these weren't the type of licks you could just hit, or you might be the one getting hit. The first one was Chief, and he was from St. Paul's. He was a Lumbee Indian, and he had Robeson County on smash. A good majority of the work in Robeson County came from him. He was a real bricklayer; to hit him was going to take some time. Then there was Drex; he wasn't all the way up like Chief, but he was comfortable. He operated on the North side of the city; his bread and butter were the trap spots he had in Bonnie Doon.

He had a spot that sold soft, and one that sold hard. Both of them did an easy fifty grand a week. The other two licks were two brothers. I considered them two different stings because they operated on different sides of town. They weren't even from Fayetteville. Their names were Lucky and Karma. They had come from Camden, New Jersey, with some heroin, and were slowly taking over. No one was really familiar with heroin in my city, but it was making a comeback. Back in the day, Fayetteville was one of the heroin capitals in the U.S., but it had fizzled out in the late 90's. Now Lucky and Karma had the market cornered. Lucky ran his operation on the eastside across the river, and Karma ran his on the westside. They were smart because every week or so, they would move their traps, making it almost impossible to catch them down bad. They were ones I really wanted to hit because they were out-of-towners.

Normally, they would've gotten ran out of town but, as I said, they were smart. Instead of eating at the table by themselves, they incorporated some local niggas in the fold. And they were feeding niggas so good that they had their loyalty and would die for the two brothers. I was going to test that theory. I really disliked up north niggas, especially New York and New Jersey niggas. They thought shit was sweet with us country boys, but it wasn't what they thought it was. And most of them came down south when they got ran from up their way. I eased from under Angie, and put my clothes back on. I pulled the covers over her, and walked outside. I had to go to the store, and get some blunts. I needed to ease my mind with some of the silver haze I had. I pulled off Redwood and onto Hope Mills Road when a police car got behind me and cut the blue lights on. Since the circle K was right there, I went ahead and pulled in.

"You got to be kidding me," I said, when I looked in the rear view mirror.

"How are you doing today, Face?" Officer Wilkins asked, walking up.

"What you stop me for?"

"Corrigan wants to talk to you," he said, and on cue Detective Corrigan pulled up beside me in a black Suburban on 26's.

He rolled the passenger side window down, and motioned for me to get in with him. It was against my better judgement, but I got out and hopped in the truck with him. He was dressed like a street nigga. He had on a big chain, rings on his fingers, and a diamond in each ear. The only way you'd know he was a cop was by the badge he wore around his neck.

"What you want, man?" I was on the edge because I was always taught that you never talked to the law.

"Miss me with the hostility." He threw a folder in my lap.

"Everything's in the folder you need to know. How you do it is up to you, but I expect twenty five percent of whatever you get."

I didn't know what he was talking about until I looked inside the folder and saw pictures of Gwap and all his info. Gwap was a hustler from Ramsey Street. I didn't know too much about him but, from skimming through the folder, I saw that he was playing with four birds. How the hell did Corrigan know that? I wasn't one to look a gift horse in the mouth, but this whole situation wasn't sitting right with me.

"I see the look on your face, so allow me to school you youngin. I'm a NARC, the head NARC to be exact. There isn't too much that goes on in this city that I don't know about. You would be surprised to find out who's a snitch. It would shake that whole belief of who's a real nigga and who isn't. See, I run down on the dope boys and give them a choice. Either pay me a monthly fee or go to prison, but sending them to prison doesn't put any money in my pockets. That's where you come in."

"So, basically, anybody who refuses—you're going to let me rob them without fear of going to jail?" I questioned.

"That pretty much sums it up and this is how we'll contact each other," he handed me a prepaid flip phone.

"Well, dig this, Corrigan, I'm gon' play your game. *But* know that I'll never tell on *anybody!* And if you play me I'll kill you."

I took the folder, and got out, not giving him a chance to respond. It was clear that he needed me more than I needed him. If they wouldn't have caught us in the house with that dead bitch, I would've laughed at him, but I kinda felt like I owed him, for not locking us up. I should've been happy that I was going to be able to operate without fear of the police, but something was telling me that I'd just got in the bed with the devil.

Nicholas Lock

Chapter Eleven

I told my brother and Murph what the deal was with Corrigan. As I expected, they were with it.

My twin was, like, "Bra, we not telling on anybody and from looking at this folder, he telling on himself. The only thing missing is who Gwap get his work from. So he been doing something wrong."

"Face, stop capping! You act like if the man came to you and said *I know everything. I got enough evidence to put you away for the next twenty years but if you pay a monthly fee you're good.* What? I'm paying!" Murph said.

"Fuck it, let's get this fetty then," I said.

"Y'all don't want nothing to eat?" Angie yelled from the kitchen.

"I want to eat you," Murph said.

"Say what?" She came into the living room.

"I'm trying to eat you," he said, and she looked at me with a raised brow. I had yet to tell them that me and Angie were a couple, but I had a feeling that they were about to find out.

"And what would my boyfriend have to say about that?" asked Angie, walking in my direction.

"Fuck that nigga! Care nothing about him."

She sat down in my lap, causing their jaws to drop.

"Oh snap!" Trip laughed.

"Now you was saying?" Angie dared.

"Fuck you," Murph grinned.

"I know it! Let's hit the streets though. Bae, you can make something to eat when we get back but right now we got to make a move." I tapped her on the butt so I could get up.

"You got off," Trip said when we got in the grey Durango I had Angie rent. "I don't understand how your ugly ass be doing it."

"Trip, y'all are identical twins! If he's ugly, that would mean you are too." Murph gave him a quizzical look.

"And she not smoking crack no more." Trip ignored Murph.

Trip continued, "But she smoking weed like it's going out of style. And since you're her nigga, you owe me for the circle I just gave her."

"We can discuss that later, I need you focused on the task at hand."

We were on the way to Gwap's spot in Tiffany Pines. If Corrigan's intel was right, we were going to come off with a nice chunk of change. I looked at the folder again to make sure I wasn't missing anything. He stayed by himself, was twenty-five, high-yellow with a slim build. In the pictures in the folder, Gwap rocked a little afro that was dyed blond on the top. He was icy in all his pictures, but there was one piece I had to get my hands on. It was a rose gold Cuban link that was about two inches wide.

"Look at this shit here, buddy," I said, as we rode by Gwap's house and saw five cars in the driveway.

"Face, I don't care if he got the president at his house. My money funny. I got lint in my pockets! This nigga getting got! I ain't going home broke tonight!" Murph emphasized his point by cocking his twin .45's, a gun he was becoming known for.

I smiled because he said five words that I hadn't heard since our B&E days. *I ain't going home broke tonight* were the words we would say to each other when we were dead set against going in the house without any money. We'd be breaking into houses all night long, trying to come up.

"I'm with Murph," Trip said.

I nodded, and pulled over down the street from Gwap's house.

"Get them zip ties out the glove compartment," I told Trip, while I pulled my ski mask down over my face. "We don't know what's what; so, if in doubt, shoot first," I added.

We got out the Durango, and used the cars in his neighbor's yard for cover as we crept up to Gwap's spot. There was music blasting inside the house, meaning we didn't have to worry about being heard. We walked beside the house, and into the backyard as the backdoor opened, and a tall dark-skinned dude stepped out. It was so dark that he didn't see us until it was too late.

"Make a noise, and you'll be at the gates of hell before your mouth closes," Trip whispered harshly, putting the Draco he was carrying in dude's face.

I zip-tied him, and asked: "How many people are inside?"

"Four," he mumbled.

Whop! I knocked him out with my choppa, and we walked inside the house. The music was coming from the front of the house. I was almost to the living room when I heard someone yell: "Stop the dice!" They were shooting Cee-lo in the living room.

Kah! Kah! I let off two rounds in the floor, while rushing into the room. "On the floor!" I yelled.

Everybody but one dude got down with their hands stretched in front of them. *Boom!* Trip shot him in the face, ending any thoughts he had of bucking. We got everybody lined up, and zip-tied. Then I grabbed Gwap, while Murph and Trip relieved them of their money.

"Ain't no need for us to play games, Gwap. You know what it is. Now where it at?" I sat him in a chair in the kitchen.

"I ain't got shit, yo. You got the wrong guy."

"Guess it's just a misunderstanding then, huh?" I lifted the Cuban links from around his neck, and dropped them in my back pocket.

I found a pot in the cabinet, filled it with water, and turned the stove eye on high. I sat the pot on the eye, and made sure I had Gwap secure in the chair.

"What are you doing?" Murph walked into the kitchen.

"About to put this nigga through the ringer."

"Wait! Huh? I told you you had the wrong guy," Gwap pleaded.

"Well, we about to find out." I grabbed the pot of boiling water, poured some of the scalding hot water in his lap, and watched as he yelled and jerked around in the chair.

"Fuck, man!" Gwap cried.

"I can do this all night, my nigga. So what you gon' do?"

"Master bedroom between the mattress," Gwap moaned out. I left him with Murph while I went to check. I found the master bedroom, and flipped the bed over, but no money. I was about to kill this nigga for playing with me. Then I saw the corner of the box spring was pulled back. I ripped it open, revealing stacks of money but no work. I found a book bag in the closet, and loaded all the money in it.

"Let's go." I walked out the backdoor, not bothering to wait for Trip and Murph.

We got back to Angie's house, and counted the money. It came up to two hundred racks. Everybody got fifty racks apiece, including Corrigan's cut. I would give him his cut tomorrow. That night, Angie got fucked on fifty thousand. That's some rich nigga shit if you ask me.

Chapter Twelve

"I knew it was something about you I liked," Corrigan said, when I gave him his cut from the Gwap sting.

"You got anybody else lined up?" I asked.

"Actually I do." He reached in the backseat, and pulled another folder out.

I grabbed it, and hopped out his Suburban. There was nothing left for us to discuss.

"What he say?" Murph asked, when I got back in my Charger.

"A bunch of nothing." I handed him the folder, and pulled off.

"Yo! You not gon' believe who it is!" Murph was excited as hell.

"Who, nigga?" He had me excited.

"Lucky." Murph referred to one of the brothers from New Jersey who had cornered the heroine market in Fayetteville.

"Karma not in there?"

"Nah," he said, flipping through the folder.

"Fuck it, he still on borrowed time." I took a hit of the weed Murph passed me.

"So you and Rai'chell done?" Murph took a swig of Hennessy VSOP straight out the bottle.

I didn't know how to answer that question. I had a soft spot for Chell, but I wasn't with the bullshit. Her nagging was too much. Nevertheless, she was still my bitch. I was just taking a break. I knew sooner or later we would get back together. We always did.

"Something like that."

"Well, you not gon' care that she fucking with Jaden?" Murph dropped the bombshell on me.

"That's on her," I shrugged, playing it cool, but I was really salty as hell.

Jaden was one of those pretty boys that played gangsta. He wasn't on the same level as me, so I couldn't understand why she would even fuck with him. Then Jaden didn't go to Douglas Byrd; he went to South View, so how they met was beyond me, but who cares. I was definitely going to holler at Diqueena about it later on, though. My iPhone buzzing took my attention.

"What up, Trip?"

"This nigga Rampage is in the mall right now, and I left my hammer at the spot!" Trip yelled into the phone.

"He seen you?" I mashed the gas.

"Nah."

"We on the way." I hung up.

"What's popping?" asked Murph.

"Rampage is in the mall as we speak," I told him, and he pulled his .45's out.

This was just what I needed to take my mind off Rai'chell's stupid ass. I sped down Hope Mills Road, and through Montclair, trying to hurry up and get to the Cross Creek Mall. It was a straight shot from where I was at. I pulled in, and got out by the food court.

"Where you at?" I called Trip.

"I'm in GameStop, and Rampage is in Reeds Jewelers in front of me."

"Okay, we walking through the food court right now." I hung up.

I pulled my snapback down as we made our way towards the jewelry store. Rampage was walking out of the store, as me and Murph bent the corner. I paused when I saw he had who I assumed was his son and girl with him. I had to give it to him, he was with the shits but he was also a coward too because the minute he saw us, he drew down. But he picked the little boy up, and used him as a shield. *Boom! Boom! Boom!* Rampage shot in our direction, forcing us to take cover. People started scattering, ducking the death being sent our way. *Boc! Boc!* I came up with my gun, returning the favor. Fuck the fact that he was holding his son! It was obvious that he didn't care about the little nigga, so why should I! *Boc! Boc!* Murph joined the fight, firing his .45s.

"Freeze!" an overweight cop said from behind us.

I turned, and sent a couple slugs his way, and he ran in the opposite direction. I knew backup was on the way, so we needed to dead Rampage asap.

"Leave him alone!" Rampage's girlfriend started peppering Murph with punches.

Wack! Murph hit her with one of his hammers, and she crumpled to the floor. Meanwhile, Rampage was weaving in and out of the crowd of people who were trying to get away from the gunfight. It was no use shooting in his direction; there were too many people in the way. Me and Murph blended in with the crowd, and made our way to my car. Rampage had ducked death this time, but next time I was going to see to it that he went to meet his maker.

Chapter Thirteen

"Why you ain't tell me Chell had a boyfriend?" I asked Diqueena.

"Because you never asked," she replied, and I threw the pillow on the couch at her.

I was chilling at Diqueena's house, giving myself a break from the madness. After the shootout we had with Rampage in the mall, he went retarded! I don't know how he found out we were from Ashton Forrest and LaFayette Village, but Rampage went on a rampage through the neighborhood, shooting shit up. My mama and Angie's house got shot up for a week straight. Every time I turned around, I was having to duck bullets. I was surprised none of us had gotten hit. Rampage was keeping it so hot on us that we hadn't had the time to hit Lucky. I had a trick for his ass, though.

"You should've just told me." I ducked the pillow she threw.

"Y'all better stop throwing my pillows," Diqueena's mom said from the kitchen.

"Okay, babymama," I said.

"Boy, hush!" Her mom chuckled.

Diqueena's mom looked exactly like Trina did when she was in her late twenties. No exaggeration. If you were to stand them beside each other, you wouldn't be able to tell them apart.

"Face, she with Jaden but you know if you call her and tell her you ready to make it work, she gon' break her neck getting here," Diqueena said.

"She broke up with me though," I informed her.

"So what? How many times y'all done broke up and made up? What's so different about this time?"

"I got a girl."

"Boy! If Rai'chell find out, I hope all hell don't break loose."

"Nah, she grown."

Diqueena shook her head.

"I'm 'bout to go, you good? You don't need anything?"

"Them new Jordans just came out," she gave me a hint.

I gave her $500, and skated off. I didn't have a problem giving Diquenna money because she was like my little sister. I hopped in the rental I was driving, since driving any of my whips was out of the question. They weren't about to catch me lacking. I headed to the eastside to meet Trip and Murph. I was supposed to have been there thirty minutes ago, but I had gotten sidetracked messing with Diqueena. I pulled into the two-story house we had rented together. When I walked in, they were loading their guns.

"It's about damn time," Murph remarked upon seeing me. I didn't respond; instead, I headed to my room to change. I had gotten the smallest room because I was rarely there. I was still staying at Angie's most of the time. I helped her get a new house in the neighborhood on Sandalwood Drive. I took off the white tracksuit I had on, and put on a black one. We were about to show Rude Boy and Rampage the error of their ways. Dope boys shouldn't beef with jackboys! A dope boy relied on hustling to eat while jackboys robbed. They would never affect our cash flow because we could always catch a D-boy lacking, but we could affect theirs, and that's exactly what we were about to do. We were about to hit one of their main trap spots, and shut that bitch down. That way, Ross could come through and open up shop, which was my initial plan anyway. We were going to give Ross Rude Boy's position.

"Y'all bums ready?" I walked down the steps.

"I stay ready so I ain't never got to get ready," my brother said.

"Let's go get this money then."

We got in Murph's rental, and headed to 301. We were going to Golden Creek, one of Rude Boy's strongholds. We pulled in, and drove to the back. We parked down the street, and watched their trap. I was hoping we would be able to catch one of the brothers lacking, and get a two for one, but their cars weren't there.

"They shit booming." Trip observed the spot.

"Better for us." I watched as fiends went in and out.

"We gon' wait a minute, so they can get a little more bread. The more cash they make, the more cash we gon' take." This statement of Murph's made sense.

"Where the bud?" I asked.

Murph pulled out some gas and rolled up. We smoked two Dutchmasters back to back, and they had me cloud- walking! My brown eyes were bloodshot and low.

"What kind of gas was that?" I needed some for myself.

"Ninety-Three Premium!" Murph said, causing us to all laugh. We were all feeling the effects of the weed. "But nah, it's called Wrong Turn."

"I need some of that after this. Y'all ready?" I asked, checking the Carbon 15 I had.

"Let's go," Trip said.

Murph drove right up to the trap, and got out. There was going to be absolutely no finesse to what we were about to do. We were out to make a statement. The fiends turned around when they saw us walking up carrying the high powered assault rifles. I walked right up to the front door, and kicked it off the hinges. Trip was the first one through the door. He shot one dude through the throat with his AR15, as the nigga scrambled to get his gun off his hip. Murph shot a nigga in the back with the SK, as the dude tried to run down the hallway. All the fiends immediately threw their hands in the air.

"Grab y'all some hard, and get the fuck out!" I told the fiends.

There was a pile of crack on the kitchen table that I assumed was what the two dead niggas were serving them from. They broke their necks grabbing the loose crack and running out. *Kah! Kah!* I shot a nigga in his leg, dropping him before he could get out the door.

"Boy, you tried that," I said.

We had been slipping! One of the niggas had blended in with the fiends, and was trying to make his way out the door, but his clothes gave him away. His were brand new, so he stuck out amongst the fiends. I don't know how we had missed him in the first place.

"You only get one chance to save your life. Where do Rude Boy and Rampage stay? And where the money?" We had been trying to find out where they stayed at, but so far the streets weren't talking.

"The money is in the bottom of the oven, and Rampage stays in Haymont Hill with his babymama. I don't know where Rude Boy stay." He groaned, holding what was left of his leg.

The Carbon 15 had knocked a chunk of his leg off. He took his last breaths, looking into my face. While Murph and Trip unloaded the money, I went to each room and set something on fire. They wouldn't be using this trap spot anymore. We went back to our duck off spot across the river to see what we had come off it with. Murph sparked another blunt of gas, as we counted the money. We all got $20,000 apiece. We decided to use the extra $5,000 to get some more hammers because when Rude Boy got wind about his trap getting shut down, he was going to try something, and I planned on being war-ready. And we had no plans of stopping. The more of his spots we hit, the funnier his money was going to look. Then we had just got the drop on Rampage. It was starting to look bad for Rude Boy.

"Yeah," I answered my phone, not recognizing the number.

"I take it you don't plan on collecting your debt," Cynthia purred in my ear.

Oh snap! Cynthia had slipped my mind.

"Honestly, Angel, I had really forgot about it. Plus that's not the way our first time should be."

She giggled. "Boy, if I didn't wanna give you no pussy, I wouldn't. Now are you coming to get this pussy or what?"

"Text me the address, and I'm on the way." I hung up.

While I was waiting on her to text me, my antennae went up. It was kinda odd that she chose now to get at me. Was she trying to set me up? I hoped she wouldn't play with her life like that.

"Bro, did you ever hook up with Cashmere?" I asked Trip.

"Did I! That Asian bitch had my toes curling, and she flexible as hell!" he bragged.

"What about you, Murph? Did you ever get up with her homegirl?"

Murph smiled. "Come on, man, this me! You know I beat her down. But the sex was so good that I left her house in a full-blown relationship."

I guess I was the only one slipping in the sex department.

"Why do you ask, my brother?" Murph said. He could smell blood in the water.

"Because Cynthia just called me."

"So you ain't hit that yet?" Murph asked incredulously.

***

The address Cynthia gave me took me to an exclusive apartment complex off Skibo Road that I had never heard of. It sat between Target and Best Buy, but it wasn't visible from the road. You had to drive around a bend to see the apartments. There was a guard booth, but it was empty at the moment. I cocked my Glock .29, and got out. I stood there, taking everything in. If this was a set-up, I was going to be ready. I refused to die before my eighteenth birthday. I kept my hand on my gun, as I made my way up the steps to her apartment. I knocked, and Cynthia answered the door in a crotchless pink teddy, looking real edible. Her shaved love box was sitting up between her legs, calling my name. She moved to the side, and let me in. I went through the house, and checked every room, closet and under the bed.

"What are you doing?" she asked.

"I had to check some shit out, come here." I sat on the edge of the bed, and she walked in between my legs.

I could relax now that I felt secure.

"You looking good as hell, Angel." I ran my hands over her perfect body.

"Why do you insist on calling me Angel?" Cynthia's green eyes were closed, while I ran my tongue over her stomach.

"Because that's what you put me in the mind of."

"You be saying all the right things." She took my head in her hands, and leaned down to kiss me.

I broke the dance our tongues were doing to take my shirt off, but Cynthia stopped me.

"I got this, you relax."

She got my shirt off, and began kissing on my neck. She pushed me back onto the bed, and worked her way down my body, leaving a trail of red lipstick. I tried to grab her butt, but she swatted my hand away. Cynthia undid my drawstring, and worked my pants down, leaving me in just my boxers. Cynthia looked me in my eyes, and pulled my swollen manhood out. She licked around the head, never taking her eyes off mine, sending chills through my body.

"Damn ma!" I grabbed the ponytail she had her hair in. Cynthia took the head of my dick into her mouth, and slowly eased me down her throat, still looking up at me.

"You not ready for this exclusive ass head game," she said, grabbing my balls, then put me back in her mouth.

I couldn't respond. Cynthia had my toes curling, she was about to suck my soul out. I had to get inside her sugar walls. I snatched her up, and threw her on the bed onto her stomach.

"Yes, daddy! That's how I want it!" she yelled, looking at me over her shoulder.

I kicked my sneakers off, and got behind her. I could see her love juices leaking on the bed. I eased my rock-hard pole between her sex lips, and thought I was in heaven. Cynthia's cat gripped me like she was made for me. I pushed in until I was balls-deep.

"Fuck!" I paused, trying not to nut.

"Kitty fire!" she bragged, wiggling beneath me.

I pulled out halfway, and pushed back in her velvet box, and painted her insides with my kids.

"Damn ma!" I said, my dick still jumping inside her.

"It's okay, daddy because I got you all night," she reassured me.

And she wasn't lying! We fucked until the sun came up, and we would have kept going, but my manhood was sore, and he wouldn't stand up no more. I went to sleep with a smile on my face. Cynthia didn't know it yet, but I was about to cuff her.

Nicholas Lock

Chapter Fourteen

Trip and Murph carried the football team to the state championship. I was mad as hell that I wasn't going to be playing, but I was happy that my niggas were, though. They were going up against the 71st Falcons, which was crazy because that was Douglas Byrd's rival. So no matter what, a Fayetteville school was going to win the North Carolina High School football championship. But I still wanted Douglas Byrd to win over 71st. The game was being held in Charlotte, North Carolina, at the Carolina Panther stadium. Me and Angie were attending the game together. We had grown closer over the last month or so. She wasn't just my woman, but she had become my voice of reason. If I did some bullshit, she was quick to call me on it.

"Damn, this shit packed!" I said to Angie, as we walked into the stadium.

"And cold." She pulled her Prada coat tighter around her.

Since dropping her habit, her caramel skin had a glow to it, and her slim-thick frame had graduated to just being thick.

"Oh my God! Hey, Face!" Some girls from school came up to me.

"What's happening?" I smiled.

"Is this your mom?" one of the girls asked, referring to Angie.

"Hell nah, this my boo." I grabbed Angie's hand, and squeezed it.

"Oh," she said and they walked off.

"Your mom, huh?" Angie looked at me.

I smiled, and grabbed her on the butt of the grey Prada jeans she had on. She swatted my hand away, and twisted her pouty pink lips up. I knew the mom comment got under her skin because Angie narrowed her eyes when the girl said it.

"You want something from the concession stand?" I asked Angie.

"A Pepsi and a burger, but walk me to our seats first."

"You not gon' stand in line with me?"

"My feet hurt, babe."

Angie had on some six-inch Prada stilettos, so I was going to give her a pass. I walked her to the luxury box I had gotten for us because I knew Angie didn't like the cold, and I wasn't trying to hear her complaining the whole time. I walked back downstairs to the concession stand, and got in line. As I stood in line, I turned and saw Diqueena. I was about to go fuck with her, but then Rai'chell walked up. I tell you, Rai'chell was looking extra good in her purple mini and thigh-high purple boots. The mini she wore hung off one of her shoulders, and hugged every curve she had. It looked as if she had put on a good ten pounds since the last time I had seen her. Diqueena looked my way, saw me, and rushed over, giving me a hug.

"Hey, bro!"

"What up?" I smiled.

"Ready for us to beat 71st so I can pop my shit to them 71st hoes. Eagle pride!" She screamed, making the 71st girls look our way. "You not gon' say nothing to my girl?" I looked at Rai'chell, and nodded, then went back to talking to Diqueena.

"Douglas Byrd deep out this bitch—It seem like the whole school here!" I said, peeping Rai'chell checking me out. I knew my drip was spilling over. I was leaving puddles everywhere I walked. I was wearing some black Dior pants, black Dior shirt, black Dior boots, and a thigh-length black Dior jacket with the hood. I had the Kobe Bryant Hublot watch on my left wrist, and a diamond bracelet on my right. Then I had rhinestone studs in my ear.

"I don't know why y'all act like y'all don't want to talk to each other." Diqueena looked at the two of us.

"I been looking for you, boo." Jaden walked up, putting his arms around Rai'chell.

Diqueena looked at me to see my reaction to Jaden hugging Chell, but I wasn't even going to trip. Why should I? He was a downgrade from me.

"I'm gon' see you later on, Diqueena," I smirked, grabbing me and Angie's food, and strolled off.

Douglas Byrd was receiving the first half kickoff when I walked back into the sky box. Keith caught the ball on the one yard line, and took it to the house, giving us an early lead.

"Eat!" I yelled, hopping around.

"Give me the food, baby, before you drop it," Angie giggled, and I kissed her.

"What was that for?"

"I didn't know I needed a reason to kiss my bitch," I said, and she raised her brows. "Okay, *my baby*." She didn't like it when I called her my bitch.

"You don't, now come sit down," she said. I was pacing around, watching the game.

"I can't, baby. I got to watch the game, this for all the marbles right here."

I couldn't lie, 71st was good as hell, but we were going for a three peat.

"I need to talk to you, baby," she said, her voice cracking. I turned around, and she walked into my arms, crying silent tears.

"What's wrong, boo?"

"Nymel, I'm too old for you," she cried, wrapping her arms around me.

At first, I was confused but now it was making sense. I knew that comment about her being my mom hadn't sat well with her.

"Baby, cut it out. You're just right for me." I tried coddling her.

"Baby, cut it out! Nymel, you're not even eighteen yet, and I'm forty-one! I'm twenty-three years older than you. We won't be able to grow old together. I don't know what I was thinking." Angie looked at me in the eye.

"Angie, what are you trying to say because to me it sounds like you're breaking up with me."

"Nymel, we can't be in a relationship, at least not in the sense of us being boyfriend and girlfriend. But that's the only thing that's going to change. This pussy still yours on command. And of course you can still stay with me if you want to, that is."

"But—" I tried to speak, but she cut me off.

"But nothing. You were there for me at my lowest, when no one else was and for that you'll always have a spot in my heart."

I didn't know how to reply to her revelation, and it seemed like she had given it a lot of thought. Even though I wanted to protest, I just said: "Okay, Angie."

We sat down and watched the game until halftime in which my boys were down two touchdowns.

"I'll be right back," I told her.

I went downstairs, and snuck into the locker room. Coach had just gotten done chewing them out when I walked in.

"Man, y'all got me bent! It's no way I busted my ass all this year to watch y'all let it go down the drain! Y'all are better than them in all aspects. I need y'all to play like it! Murph, that left tackle is weak, a bull rush will beat him every time. And Trip, the left cornerback is playing flat footed, and he's sitting on the curl route. So an out and up by Sherman is a guaranteed six points." I gave them what I was seeing. "Win on three. One, two, three! *Win!*"

I went back to the box with Angie, and watched as we came back to win by two touchdowns. The coach let me take the championship photo with the team. My football career was officially over, but my robbing career was just getting started!

Nicholas Lock

Chapter Fifteen

We had had enough days off. It was time for us to get back to work. Tonight I was going to see how *lucky* Lucky was. We were all at the spot across the river, which was also the side of town that Lucky ran his operation from. Without Corrigan it would've probably taken us some months to get a bead on Lucky. He switched his traps up too much, but none of that was going to matter tonight. We had the address to Lucky's main residence, so we weren't concerned with his traps, at least I wasn't.

"It's no way we can pass up hitting the trap in Cat Tail," Murph said.

"Shitting me if it's no way. The big money is at his house, bro." I tried reasoning with Murph.

"I can guarantee you it's a lot of money in his trap too," he continued.

"How?"

"Look at this," Murph handed me his phone.

I looked at the touchscreen and the video that was playing. It was showing a trailer that had a non stop flow of traffic. When I say non-stop I mean non-stop.

"That's Lucky's spot in Cat Tail. Face, I'm willing to bet that they sitting on an easy hundred bands. That flow you're seeing is all day every day. *Jack or die*, remember?" He hit me with my shit.

Murph had a point. I just hated doing shit spur of the moment. I liked for shit to be mapped out for the most part. Then Cat Tail had an added element of risk because it was one way in and one way out. I wasn't trying to get trapped off. But Murph wanted to do it, so that's what it was. There was no set leader amongst us, so everybody's voice and opinion held the same amount of weight.

"Where the hell Tyrone at?" Trip asked, ready to get it in.

Trip wasn't going to be with us much longer. He was graduating early so he could enroll in college before the spring semester. Trip wanted to catch spring conditioning at UNC. He was the number one rated dual quarterback in the nation. They were predicting the Tar Heels to make a run at the College Football playoffs. This was going to be our last sting together.

"Here he go right here," Murph opened the door, allowing Tyrone to come in.

Tyrone was our plug on the guns. He was in the army, so he had access to any gun you could think of. Tyrone was dark brown, about 5'10, and stocky. He kept his hair cut real low, and stayed with a pair of designer shades covering his eyes. At twenty-one he had been in the army for three years, he said he was getting out next year.

"Y'all not gon' help?" Tyrone asked, lugging two green duffel bags.

"Damn! What's in here?" Trip almost dropped the bag he grabbed.

"You ain't got to ask that," said Tyrone.

They put the duffel bags on the kitchen table, and opened them up. I immediately got nervous, and started sweating! Tyrone had grenades and all in the bag.

"These mine right here," Murph grabbed two Taurus .45s out the bag.

I reached in the bag, and pulled out a camouflage Mini .14 with a scope on it.

"Check this out," Tyrone reached over and hit a button on the mini .14, and a green light came on. "Anything you put that light on is getting hit. And I'm gon' throw some tracer rounds in, free of charge.

Murph grabbed something called a CZ Scorpion Evo 3 submachine gun. It was about as long as my forearm.

"She shoots .9 and .223 rounds," said Tyrone.

I reached in the other bag, and pulled out a bullet-proof vest.

"That will stop an AK-47 bullet," Tyrone informed me. Both Trip and Murph grabbed one too.

Then I grabbed a 10mm Springfield, some extra clips, and put it on my hip.

"Y'all about to go to war or something?" Tyrone questioned, seeing the way we were strapped up.

"Nah, but to get caught lacking is against our religion," said Trip, grabbing a M16.

Tyrone nodded as if he understood. Tyrone was one of our niggas for real, but he wasn't participating in what we were about to do, so it was of no use for him to know. Had Murph or even Trip been on the outside looking in, I wouldn't have told them either. We paid bro, and he left.

"So what y'all want to hit first? The trap or Lucky's house?" Trip questioned.

I quickly replied: "Lucky's house. That way, we can hit the trap and won't have to drive too far to the house."

We donned the bullet-proof vests, and got in a black Charger that we gave a fiend half an ounce of hard to use. I cut on Pop Smoke's street banga, "Shake The Room"— featuring Quavo—and rode out. Lucky stayed in Raeford, a city on the outskirts of Fayetteville. I figured Lucky was doing good, but the house said he was doing damn good! It didn't matter if you were rich or poor, you knew money when you saw it, and when you'd seen Lucky's house you knew it cost money. It was a large two-story house made of white bricks, with palm trees scattered throughout the property. There were marble statues of the number seven by the massive front door. Lucky had big flood lights all around his house so even though it was nine o'clock at night, Lucky's yard was lit up like it was midday. There were two two-car garages connected to differ-ent ends of the house. One of the garages was open, revealing a Ferrari and an Acura NSX. The driveway was shaped like a T, with white bricks leading up to the all glass front door.

"This nigga got that bread!" Murph said.

"How in the hell are we going to get into the house?" Trip asked.

"Y'all niggas ain't got no faith in your boy," I feigned hurt.

I parked at the house next door, which I found out was empty from my previous trip to scope things out. We checked our weapons, and got out.

"I know I don't have to give y'all no speech about what we're about to do, so let's leave this nigga dead minus his bread," I said.

As we approached the side of his house, it started raining and thundering.

"Bullshit!" Murph's pretty boy ass said. "I just got these." His stupid ass had worn some black suede Chanel sneakers.

"I'm sorry to see that," Trip chuckled.

Where Murph thought the thunderstorm was bad, I thought it couldn't have come at a better time. The drenching rain would make us nearly invisible to cameras if he had any. I pulled the .10mm out, and waited. The minute it thundered, I aimed and shot at the flood lights, bathing the side of the house in darkness. I knew Lucky was a street nigga, so I wasn't worried about him having any live-in security. I was more worried about him getting wind of what was happening before we had a chance to get our hands on him.

"Y'all hear that?" Trip asked.

"What?" I asked, then I heard it, and my heart dropped. I ain't letting Lucky leave. I ran around the side of the house as Lucky was backing his Ferrari out the garage. I tucked the

.10mm, and brought the mini 14 up. *Tat! Tat! Tat! Tat!* I shot the Ferrari's tires out, preventing him from going any further. *Doon! Doon! Doon!* Murph shot the car up.

"No! No!" I shouted. "Don't kill the nigga yet!"

I ran over to the Ferrari, and yanked the door open. Lucky was holding his face with blood all over his hands. I thought Murph had shot him in the face. I looked closer, and saw the blood was coming from the cuts and gashes on his face from the glass shattering.

"Fuck, man!" Lucky yelled, when I yanked him from the car.

"Shut up!" I dragged him into the garage.

I wasn't worried about anybody calling the police because the shots were muffled by the constant thunder. Me and Trip carried Lucky in the house, while Murph drove the car back into the garage. We sat him down on the kitchen floor.

"Do y'all know who the fuck y'all are messing with?" Lucky growled, wiping the blood out of his eyes.

"We do, Lucky, so that should tell you all you need to know," Trip said.

"I thought you were going to the store, baby?" A white chick came into the kitchen, holding a newborn baby.

"Run, Kelly!" Lucky yelled.

"No, you don't, bitch" Murph grabbed her by her ponytail, before she could get anywhere.

"I'm gon' tell you like I tell everyone else—Make it easy on me and you, and tell me where the money and work at," I said.

"You think I would keep some drugs here?" Lucky replied, and earned himself a kick to the face.

"Leave us alone!" his girl pleaded.

"So where the money at then?" I ignored her.

"You're a dead man! I'll let your family live if you leave now."

"Ha-ha-ha! You're either delusional or you have the heart of a lion," I said.

"I got this," Murph grinned.

Murph walked over to Lucky's bitch, and snatched the newborn out of her hands, causing him to cry.

"Give me my baby!" She tried to get at Murph, but Trip grabbed her.

"Let her go, bra," I said, and shot her in the face.

I looked down at Lucky's husky frame, and took a step back. We hadn't tied him up, and I didn't need him getting desperate and trying anything. Lucky was the same height as me, and about the same size, so I wasn't into wrestling with him. We didn't have on any masks, so no one was walking out but us. I watched as Murph went to the oven and cut it on 500 degrees. I knew where this was going. I knew my nigga was retarded, but he was getting downright heartless.

"What's it gon' be?" Murph asked, placing the baby in the preheating oven.

"The safe! The safe! Under the fish tank!" Lucky yelled. "42, 40, 42, 16!" He yelled the combo out.

Murph took the baby out the oven, and started rocking him, trying to get him quiet. Murph was on Dr. Jekyll and Mr. Hyde shit! Trip watched Lucky while I went to check the safe. I found the fish tank in the living room, and it was huge! It covered the entire wall. I opened the bottom and, sure enough, there was a titanium safe built into the bottom. I put the combination in; it clicked, and I pulled the door open. Oh my God!

Chapter Sixteen

I knew immediately that it was at least a million dollars in the safe. The bundles of cash were neatly on top of each other. I walked back into the kitchen behind Lucky, and put a round through the back of his head, spraying Trip with blood and brain matter.

"The fuck!" Trip got mad.

"Shut up and come here," I said, walking back into the living room.

"Bra, what you got going on?" I questioned Murph when I saw he still had the baby in his arms.

"What am I supposed to do?" he asked me.

I really didn't have an answer. I was cold-blooded, but I wasn't into harming kids, so I shrugged. I had a more pressing matter. While me and Murph were talking, Trip had found some bags, and was emptying the safe. I ran next door, and brought the car over. Trip had the bags waiting at the door. It had stopped raining, so we didn't have to rush loading the bags in. I hadn't searched Lucky's room, and there was no way I was going to leave his or his bitch's jewelry in the house. I was headed to the master bedroom when Murph walked past me, wearing a neck full of chains and rings on every finger with the baby still in his arms. So I knew he had beat me to the punch.

"We dropping that baby off at the hospital, mother goose." I picked at Murph because he hadn't put the little nigga down since grabbing him. I think he felt bad about the oven thing, but that was Lucky's fault.

"Fuck you," he smiled.

I did the speed limit all the way back to Fayetteville. I couldn't afford to get pulled for speeding, even though I wanted to put the pedal to the metal. I couldn't wait to count up the money from the safe.

"Pull your hoody over your head and lay the nigga by the emergency door." I looked in the backseat at Murph. He opened the door, and ran to drop the baby off.

"Yo, there goes Rampage's Camaro!" Trip pointed.

I looked and, sure enough, Rampage was driving down Owen Drive, headed towards 301.

I got out, and got in the backseat.

"Hurry up, nigga! Rampage just rode by!" I said impatiently, as we pulled out of Cape Fear Valley Medical Center, and got stuck at the intersection of Owen Drive and Village Drive.

"Fuck!" Murph beat the steering wheel.

"Chill, there he go pulling into the ABC store." I pointed.

The light turned green, and we pulled into the ABC store parking lot.

"Park beside him," I said.

I rolled the back window down, and waited for Rampage to come out. Tonight was turning out to be a good one. We might be able to pull a three-in-one combo. Rampage came out the the liquor store with a bottle of 1942 in his hand, and his phone to his ear. He paid the Charger no mind, as he approached. I brought the mini 14 up when he got to his car, and let her talk. *Tat! Tat! Tat!* The high-powered rounds caught him in his neck and upper chest area, knocking his head clean off his shoulders.

Skaaa! We burnt rubber, getting away from the crime scene. I texted Ross to let him know that we no longer had to worry about anyone going on any rampages. He would understand.

"We still gon' hit Cat Tail," Murph stated.

"Bra, are you serious?" I wondered.

"Is a pig's pussy pork?" he replied.

"Whatever," I sighed.

I honestly didn't want to, if I was being truthful, but my nigga had his mind made up. I looked out the window at the Christmas lights decorating the houses. It was almost Christmas time, and I couldn't think of one that was going to be as good as this one. Looking at the bags full of money solidified that.

"We in and out," I said seriously.

We turned in Cat Tail, and cruised through. I saw different dudes standing around at different trailers. It was cold as hell out, and the thunderstorm had dropped the temperature to a T, but niggas was still out chasing paper. The trailer we were going to hit was bumping! I could see why Murph was set on hitting it.

"Look, the flow is so constant that we'll be able to just walk in like everybody else. Trip, you go to the back door in case someone tries to go out that way." I laid the plan out.

Murph pulled right up to the trap, and we got out. Trip ran around the back while we went through the front door. It wasn't hard to distinguish who was selling and who was copping, by their dress code.

"You know what it is! Time to pay the piper," I said to the two young niggas that was passing out bags.

There was always a stupid nigga in the crew; but me knowing this, I was ready. So when one of the dudes went for his pistol, the Springfield in my hand jumped, sending two hollow points in his face. The other one threw his hands in the air, and said, "The dope is in the cereal boxes."

I looked on top of the refrigerator, and saw five boxes of frosted flakes. *Kalt! Kalt!* I heard Trip's M16 go off, and I looked down the hallway, and I saw a short bald headed dude lying dead by the back door with a duffel bag in his hands. I don't know what I was thinking by not checking the trailer. Trip had saved us. While all of this was taking place, all the junkies had scattered. *Boom!* Murph shot the young boy in the face. Trip grabbed the duffel bag by the back door, and me and Murph grabbed the cereal boxes. We got back to the car at the same time, with Trip in the driver seat and Murph in the passenger seat.

"I told you niggas the shit was gonna be sweet!" Murph said.

But he had spoken too soon because bullets started pinging the Charger. I grabbed the mini 14, and began firing back. I shot the back window out, and let the assault rifle do its thing. There was niggas shooting at us from everywhere! I even think the junkies were shooting at us!

"Murph!" Trip yelled.

I turned to see Murph slumped forward in the passenger seat with blood coming out of the top of his head. I wanted to check on him, but I could not stop shooting or they would really shoot our shit up. With me shooting back, they had to keep ducking off.

"Get us out of here!" I yelled, grabbing Trip's M16, and letting off. I ran out of bullets just as we made it out of Cat Tail. I checked on Murph, and saw he was still breathing. I called Angie, and told her to get to our house and bring some medical equipment because Murph had gotten shot. We couldn't take him to the hospital; that was out of the question. We got to the house, and we got Murph's unconscious ass in the house. I grabbed a wet rag, cleaned some of the blood off his head, and said: "Man, wake your bitch ass up."

The bullet hadn't gone in; it was only a graze. He was going to need some stitches, but he was going to be okay. He had us thinking he was on the brink of death. Angie came and stitched Murph up, and asked a hundred and one questions.

While that was taking place, me and Trip started counting money. Lucky had made it easy for us because every bundle of money was twenty thousand, and there were a hundred bundles equaling two mill. We would all get half a mil apiece, and we hadn't counted the money from hitting the trap yet. I had already made my mind up that Corrigan wasn't going to get a cut of the trap money. We counted the trap money, and it equaled up to three hundred racks, putting me, Trips and Murph's out to six hundred thousand. Not to mention the two bricks of heroin we got. We were all the way up! We were half millionaires, and hadn't reached eighteen yet, so you know what I was about to do—Stunt!

Nicholas Lock

Chapter Seventeen

"Face, you're making me a wealthy man! At this rate I'll be able to retire in the next few years," Corrigan told me.

We were once again in his Suburban, and I had just given him his cut of the money.

"Retire?"

"Yeah, retire. You don't think I'm gonna be doing this my whole life. You better get you an exit plan too."

"I'm good. I'm gon' be robbing these suckers until my casket closes. Niggas like me don't retire."

He laughed at my statement. "Oh, they retire but it's not by choice. They retire to the penitentiary and the grave. The faster your young ass realize that, the better off you'll be. Do you know how many niggas I've put away for twenty plus years?"

Corrigan's question snapped me back to reality. I had forgot that the bitch ass nigga was still a cop, a street nigga's most hated enemy. I was blinded by the fact that he was lacing my pockets. It was time for me to start using him the same way that he was using me. It's crazy how money could bring sworn enemies together.

"You need to go down the path your brother is going. I took you for the thinker, but I might've been wrong. College is the way to go." Those words of his let me know he knew more about me than I knew about him. I was going to change that, though.

"You don't have a folder for me?" I was ready to get away from him.

"Slow down and enjoy yourself. You just hit for half a mil. I'll have something for you in a few days."

I got out of his truck, and into my Charger. I had gotten it fixed from Rampage shooting it up. Since Rampage's demise,

Rude Boy had been quiet. Ross had taken over Golden Creek with no problem, but I knew it wasn't over unless Rude Boy was just a straight up buster. And if that was the case, making Ross the king of 301 was going to be easier than I thought. I called Cynthia to see if she was ready. Me and Cynthia had become an item. Once I sat down with her, I realized she was cool as a fan; she was just spoiled as hell. Both of her parents had lucrative careers. Her mother was a heart surgeon, and her dad was a judge, and they gave her whatever she wanted—especially her dad. She was a real daddy's girl; she even had *daddy's girl* tattooed on the left side of her neck.

"You ready, bae?" I was getting ready to go shopping, and I was letting her tag along.

"I'm waiting on you."

"Come outside in fifteen minutes." I hung up.

We were about to hit the SouthPark Mall in Charlotte. Me, Trip and Murph were hitting the club tonight. Trip was leaving tomorrow for Chapel Hill, and we were going to celebrate tonight. I was gon' be sad to see my twin leave, but it was gonna be for the best. His heart wasn't really into the streets. Football was his life. When I pulled up to Cynthia's apartment, she was outside, leaning against her Lexus LC 500. Shorty was bad! I don't know how Rude Boy let her get away. Cynthia had on a form-fitting yellow and black Cushnie dress and some yellow Giuseppe Zanotti slingbacks. Her hair was pulled up in a Chinese bun.

"God made you with me in mind," I said, admiring her hourglass shape.

"Hello to you too, handsome." She placed a passionate kiss on my lips. I pulled off with her holding my hand.

"Nymel, I don't know what it is but I'm really digging your young ass. I can see us at the altar exchanging wedding vows. I even told my daddy about you." She rubbed my thigh.

"You don't know what it is, huh?" I looked in her green eyes.

"I don't mean it like that, boo, because I do know what it is. It's just—"

"Just what?" I questioned as I drove.

"Rude Boy hurt me bad, Nymel. I can't afford to be put through that again." She sighed.

"You know me better than that, don't you?" I was digging her too.

"That's what's so perplexing to me. I've only known you for a few months, and I feel like I've known you my whole life. And you treat me so damn good." Cynthia beamed. "I can honestly say that I know you won't do me dirty, which is why I stopped taking my birth control. I want your baby. But it is something I need to tell you."

"What?" I was hoping she didn't say anything that was going to make me pull over and make her get out my whip.

"I knew who you were the first time we met. I saw your picture in Rude Boy's Hummer, and I heard him and Rampage talking about killing you."

"When was this?"

"Damn, let me finish, bae. Anyway though, when you approached me, I was gonna tell Rude, but the way you came at me intrigued me. All that talk about treating me like an angel struck a nerve. Then we met up, and you really treated me like an angel." She rubbed on my thigh. "You're mature for your age. You act like someone ten years older. Baby, you also need to watch out for Black."

"Who is Black?" I didn't know him.

"He's the brother of Reese, and Rude Boy's cousin; you obviously killed him." Cynthia just told me something that was new to me.

To my understanding I hadn't killed anybody named Reese, but when bullets start flying, I don't ask names. Cynthia must've known I was confused because she said, "The only reason that they know it was you is because when you came shooting in Taylors Creek, you supposedly dropped a gold AK that was Reese's."

Oh shit! Reese was the dark-skinned nigga that I had killed that day at D.J's house when we robbed him.

"What does Black look like?" I needed to know.

"He's dark-skinned, kinda fat with a temp fade." She described the dude that Rampage had pointed us out to at the South View football game.

Fuck him! If he wanted smoke, I didn't have a problem giving it to him. I had to warn Murph and Trip about this nigga, so they wouldn't get caught lacking.

"So when am I gon' meet your parents?" I changed the subject.

"Oh my gosh! Are you serious? Because I'll set it up immediately." Cynthia was excited.

"Go ahead and set it up."

"I love you, baby." She pecked me on the cheek.

"Love you too," I told her, as she reached for my zipper and blessed me with some top-notch brain before we got to Charlotte.

***

"Where you going all dressed up?" Angie was lying across the bed, watching me get all dripped up.

"You know Trip going off to college tomorrow so we about to celebrate," I said, putting on the rose gold Carolina Panther chain I had robbed the nigga Gwap for.

I wasn't really the clubbing type. I was content just being around my niggas or some females. I was really antisocial if I was keeping it real. Plus being around a bunch of people made me edgy, then it made me put some liquor in my system, and I got down right mean. But tonight was cause for a celebration, so I was gonna chill. I looked myself over, and was thoroughly impressed. I had snapped out of my mind in the mall! I had on some white fitted Gucci jeans with the knees shredded open. Under the jeans, I had on some gold thermals that you could see through the knees of the Gucci jeans. Then I brought a white Gucci thermal with gold G's all over it. On my feet I had on some high designer white and gold sneakers. I had a pinky ring on both pinkies, and four carats in each ear. I had finished the outfit off with a pair of white and gold Gucci glasses.

"Be safe, baby," she said.

"You trying to come?" I sat down on the bed, and palmed her ass through the lace boy shorts she was wearing.

"No, boy, and you better stop before you start something you can't finish." Angie grinned.

"I finish everything I start, don't try me!" I warned.

Me and Angie still fucked on the regular, and I still stayed with her if I wasn't at the house across the river, or at Cynthia's. I got up off the bed, and was headed out of the door when Angie said: " Tell Trip and Murph I said *Hey*."

"Bye, woman."

I walked out and hopped in my new black R8 GT. My brother and Murph were going to trip out when they saw my new car. We were meeting at *Club Platinum*, a spot that had opened recently on Bragg Boulevard. I leaned my seat back, and lit the half blunt of kush in the parking lot. I saw Trip and Murph standing by two foreigns.

"Whose shits is them?" I asked, hopping out.

"Don't carry us," Trip said, leaning up against a white Maserati Granturismo Sport.

"Yea, nigga," Murph said, running his hand across the red Aston Martin Vantage.

I tell you, the foreigns were dead fresh. Trip had on a purple and black Fendi outfit, and Murph was rocking some red Versace pants, white Versace polo, and some red and white Christian Louboutin boots. We looked like money walking up to the door.

"Uh un! You not leaving us in this line," Tessa said to Murph.

"Come on," he said.

Tessa, Kay-Kay, and their sister—Bria—followed us to the door. We paid the bouncer a fee for skipping the line, and walked in. I was checking Kay-Kay sexy red ass out. All three sisters were bad, but Kay-Kay was winning. Kay-Kay was about 5'6", thick thighs, big butt, no titties. Her silky jet-black hair fell about three inches below her shoulders.

"Damn, nigga!" Kay-Kay said, catching me staring.

I didn't say nothing. I walked up to the steps to VIP instead. There were bottles of Hennessy and Patron with ice in buckets. We started popping bottles, and cutting up, having a good time in general. It was my brother's last night in the city, and we were going to turn up! Megan Thee Stallion's hit—*Body*—came on, and the sisters started twerking. I sat back, and watched them get it in, particularly Kay-Kay. I wanted to holler, but I had enough pussy in my life at the moment. Besides, Kay-Kay was ratchet, and I didn't want her and my lady to get to beefing. I was gon' get her number, though. I had just got behind Kay-Kay while she was throwing that ass when Murph tapped me on the shoulder, and whispered in my ear. "That nigga Black just came in and they deep."

I hated to fuck up my brother's celebration night, but it was what it was. I walked out of the VIP and up to Black.

"I heard you been looking for me," I said.

"Nigga, you know what's up." He had a deep voice like Barry White. He'd said enough. I swung the Hennessy bottle, and hit Black in the side of the head; he was asleep before his body hit the ground. I was about to stomp him out when one of his boys punched me in the mouth. The club turned into a free-for-all. My twin hit him in the head, staggering him, then Murph followed up and dropped him. Everybody started fighting! It was no longer just us versus them. It looked like the whole club was fighting. With Black and his boys outnumbering us five to one, it worked out in our favor. They not only had to fight us, but everybody else as well. I looked out of the corner of my eye and saw Kay-Kay and her sister beating the shit out of Tamara. The bouncers started spraying mace, causing everybody to try and get outside. As we made our way outside, Ross was riding up with Sha Loc, another one of my niggas from the hood.

"Yea! What's up now, nigga! You snuck me in the club, pussy!" I looked back and saw Black emerging from the club and headed my way with his shirt off.

Was this nigga serious? I had put his brother on the front of a t-shirt and knocked him out in the club and he was trying to fight? Now fighting was right up my alley. I was with that, but I was dripping a little bit too much to do some fighting at the moment. I think Sha Loc knew it too because he came out the window with a .50 cal Desert Eagle. He started busting in Black's direction, causing everybody to get low and run to their cars. Black turned to run, and the first slug from the D.E. spun him back around facing us. The next two rounds from the high caliber gun hit Black square in the forehead, sending half his head onto the windshield of a passing car. I ran to my car, reached in my pocket for the keys, but they were gone. Meanwhile, Trip and Murph were driving off. Then my door clicked and opened. I looked inside, and Kay-Kay was sitting in the passenger seat.

"What are you doing in my car? I mean, how did you get my keys?" I asked, getting behind the wheel.

"When you left out of VIP, your keys were on the table, so I grabbed them. I didn't see you when I got outside, so I came to your car. All of a sudden, somebody started shooting, and I got in. You want me to get out or something, dang!" She had a look on her face, like: *what, nigga!*

"Shut the hell up, girl!" I pulled off. There were sirens in the distance.

"Tell your mama to shut up."

I started laughing. "Don't make me fuck you up."

"You better do it right," Kay-Kay replied, and I looked over at her.

"Boy, what you looking at? Hurry up so you can eat this pussy," her ratchet ass said.

I drove to the Hilton like I was Jeff Gordon. No words were spoken for the rest of the night. The only sounds coming out of the room we were in were moans and grunts.

Chapter Eighteen

I was bored as hell, cruising through the city, blowing on some white kush. Every time I pulled on the blunt, I would cough, but the potent weed had me out of my mind. It was a bright, cloudless day, and the sun had it feeling like it was summer instead of winter.

Trip was off to college and Murph was laid up with Vanessa. Since I had wifed Cynthia up, Murph had wifed up Vanessa. I found myself pulling into Golden Creek. After we hit Rude Boy's trap and burned it down, Ross had come through and finished it up by running the rest of Rude Boy's soldiers and hustlers out. All that was left was Ross's crew, and niggas who had no hand in the beef but were from the neighborhood. Ross now had a good portion of 301 in his pocket. If he could get Taylor's Creek under his thumb, then Ross would control the majority of 301 that ran through Fayetteville. I pulled onto the backstreet, and parked in front of Ross's weed spot. The steady flow of traffic over at the heroin spot let me know the work we got from Lucky was good money. Ross had three traps on the same street. Two of them were right beside each other, which were the crack/powder spot and the heroin spot. The weed spot was directly across the street. It was a good set-up because to try and rob one would be suicide. The people in the other two traps would be on your ass before you could get back out the house. Unless you were me, of course.

When I got out the Charger, two dudes stepped out of the powder spot, and mugged me. I pulled my hood on, and tucked my hands inside the grey Nike hoody I had on. I smirked at the dudes mean-mugging me, and walked up to the weed spot. The added weight on my hip from the .357 Glock kept me worry-free. If they started to act crazy, I was gonna show them

I didn't act crazy. I was. When I got up the steps, Ross was standing in the door, smiling.

"What's happening?" I asked.

"This money. I saw you antagonizing my little niggas across the street too." He dapped me up.

"They did that to themselves rocking them dumb ass mean mugs. I ain't never known no mean mug to kill anybody, but how many niggas you think done got killed because they was mean-mugging a nigga?"

"A lot." Sha Loc came out the back with a fat blunt between his lips, and no shirt.

Sha Loc was 5'9, light brown-skinned, about 190 pounds, with a fade. He was big on working out, so he was cut up like a bad bag of dope, and he almost never had a shirt on. If he didn't have to wear a shirt, he didn't. Sha Loc had been staying in Ashton Forrest since he was a boy too, so he was another one of our niggas. He was just crazy as hell!

"Go put a shirt on," I said. "I appreciate what you did the other night too."

"Come on, cuz, you already know." He passed me the blunt he was blowing on.

Ross addressed me as I smoked the blunt. "Face, you know I don't really deal with that boy like that, but that shit got the fiends going dumb! You get your hands on some more, hit me asap. I'll probably be out in the next few days."

"Say what! I need that!" Sha Loc hung his Galaxy up.

"What you talking about?" Ross inquired.

Sha Loc replied. "You know the brothers Lucky and Karma? Well, Lucky got his wig split and he's no longer with us, so Karma is saying he has a million dollars for the body of whoever is responsible. And if you can get them alive, he's paying three million. I told you them niggas had that bread."

This was perfect, I thought to myself. Karma was serving himself to me on a silver platter. I could bring him anybody and say it was them.

"How he gon' know if it's the right person or not?" I needed to know.

"I asked that and he said he'll know, so whatever that means—" Sha Loc shrugged.

What the fuck did they mean he'll know? Had there been some cameras I hadn't seen or something? It was no way he knew it was us, or he'd be saying our names. Then again, if he was smart, he would put two and two together and realize that whoever had killed Lucky was more than likely the same people who had robbed Lucky's trap. I had to get at Karma before it got out that it was us. Half the city would be gunning for us for a million dollars. For three million I could see the entire city trying to catch us lacking, and that included family and friends.

"Damn, cuz, you gon' smoke the whole blunt?" Sha Loc asked me.

I laughed, and passed him the blunt. "I'm gon' catch up to y'all later. I need to handle something."

I dapped my niggas up, and went to set my plan in motion.

To do what I needed to do, I needed to catch Karma lacking. Lucky's funeral would've been the perfect spot, but they were having the funeral in New Jersey. There was always Lucky's girlfriend's funeral, but I had an even better solution. If the brothers were as close as I thought they were, then Karma wasn't going to allow his nephew to become a ward off the state. That was going to lead me straight to Karma.

I walked into the social services building, found the floor I was looking for, and got on the elevator. *I had to be the luckiest nigga alive*, I said to myself when I saw who was behind the reception desk. It was Laci, a heavy-set caramel girl that I went to school with. I had been a freshman, and she had been a junior. She wasn't ugly by far. She kept her hair and nails done, and was an all-around cool chick. We had chopped it up a few times when she was the manager for the football team. But she was just way too big! Laci was about 5'5 and probably 200 pounds.

"Boy, what are you doing in here?" Laci asked me.

"How you know I ain't here looking for you?" I asked, and she rolled her eyes.

"I'm not your type, Nymel, so quit playing, let me give you directions to where you need to go," her mouth said, but her eyes told me to keep going.

"I need an address."

"An address?" Laci looked at me curiously.

"Yea. I know y'all had a baby boy to come in, and I'm trying to find out who came and got him and what their address is." I told the half-truth.

"You know that's against the rules. I ain't about to lose my job messing with these white people shit."

"Come on, Laci, I'd owe you one," I begged. "Do this for me, and I'll treat you to an entire day of pampering. I'm talking hair, feet, nails, massages and all." I would have given up a lot more for Karma's address.

"You can't renege on me either." Laci pointed her red nails at me, and started typing on the computer in front of her.

"Her name is Barbara Jenkins, she's listed as the grandmother."

"That's the only name you see?"

"Next of kin is Karmal Jenkins, he's listed as an uncle," Laci informed me.

"What's their info?"

I wrote down Karma's info, and gave Laci my info so she could call me and let me know when she wanted her pampering. I wasn't tripping because the money that I was about to hit Karma for would overshadow the money I was going to spend getting her pampered.

Nicholas Lock

Chapter Nineteen

"Bra, this is a fake address—There's no way Karma lives here," Murph said.

Murph could be right because the brick house wasn't anything spectacular, and the neighborhood wasn't known for luxury. Ponderosa was basically a middle-class subdivision where a lot of hood motherfuckas stayed. We had been watching the house from the neighbor's for the last three days, and hadn't seen a single soul. So, unless we were watching at the wrong times, then the house was empty. I had decided the house was a dead end, and was about to pull off when Murph stopped me.

"Check it out," he pointed to a red G-wagon coming down the street.

Now Ponderosa wasn't the ghetto, but a red Mercedes truck on some rims that cost a fortune spoke volumes. That was a red flag. We leaned down in our seats, as the truck passed us and cruised down the street, bypassing the house. Then the tint on the truck prevented us from seeing inside.

"I should've known our luck wasn't that good." Murph sat back up.

"They're coming back," I said, looking in the rearview mirror.

The truck came down the street, and pulled into the driveway of Karma's address. If Karma got out the truck, he would be dead or dying before he could get his key in the door. Instead, a young boy hopped out. I had never seen him before. He was tall, about 6'3, slim, brown-skinned, with a high top fade. His jewels let me know he was getting to the money. He had on three big ropes, two bracelets on each wrist, and a big-faced watch. I was too far away to tell what it is.

"That nigga ain't even got no strap." Murph eyed the young boy.

"How you know?"

"Where would it be, smart guy?" Murph hadn't taken his eyes off him.

Murph was right because the tight shirt and skinny jeans the nigga was wearing would've shown a bulge somewhere.

"You ready?" I asked.

"When am I not?" he replied.

We got out, and rushed up to the house. In his haste to get in the house, the young boy hadn't closed the door all the way. We walked in the house, into the living room, and it was empty except for a couch and a coffee table. I could hear the young boy down the hall somewhere talking.

"Karma, how much I'm supposed to grab? A'ight give me fifteen."

He was hanging up when me and Murph strolled in the room, causing him to piss on himself.

"No way!" Murph yelled, doubling over, laughing.

"Damn, homey!" I said, looking at the dark spot in front of his pants.

"Oh shit!" Murph peeked in the closet.

I moved into the room some more, so I could see what had caught Murph's attention. I had been standing in the doorway.

"Oh, Karma gon' kill you! You let us catch you lacking in his stash spot." I shook my head.

The seriousness of the situation must've dawned on him because he tried to kick the safe door closed, but Murph threw him across the room.

"The next time you move, somebody gon' be trying to console your grieving mother," Murph told him.

The closet had a safe in the corner that was just as tall as I was, and the whole thing was filled with bricks of dog food.

There had to be at least fifty bricks, and that was me taking a guess.

Why Karma gave this address to social services was a mystery to me. Murph grabbed the bag off the floor that the young boy had dropped, and started placing bricks inside.

"Karma is gon' hunt you niggas to the end of the earth for this," the young nigga told us.

"How he gon' do that, pissy? He don't know who we are, but what he gon' do to you is the real question. That really doesn't concern me, though. I'll make a deal with you. If you tell me where Karma stay, I'll make it look good on you."

"I ain't telling you crab ass niggas shit!"

The way he was talking, you would have never guessed that this was the same nigga that we had just scared the piss out of.

"What if your life depended on it?" Murph put a .45 to his head.

"You would just have to kill me."

I chuckled. "You got a set of nuts on you. You're lucky I'm not in the mood to get bloody because if I was on my bull-shit, I would make you swallow them. Literally. Yo, what I don't understand is how you're willing to die for an out-of-town nigga. You don't got no up north accent, so you got to be a Fayetteville nigga but you jacking they lingo. We don't call niggas crabs unless you're on some gang shit." I wanted to kill him, but I needed him.

"Give me your phone, close your eyes, and count to three hundred. If I see your eyes before we leave, I'll be the last person you see." The tone of my voice was menacing.

I picked up one of the bags of heroin, and almost dropped it. The bag was heavy as hell. I looked and saw Murph with a small bag in his hands, trying to hold his laugh in. I gave him

125

the finger, and walked to the car. I sped off. I had to get the mandatory life sentence that was in the bags out of my car.

"Boy, that nigga bitch got a fat pussy," Murph said.

I looked over and saw him looking through the young boy's phone. I had meant to throw it out the window when I had turned out of Ponderosa.

"Man, get that hot ass phone out my car!" I snatched the phone, rolled my window down and slung the phone out.

"You should have let me get the bitch number first, damn!" Murph said.

I had to laugh, my nigga was silly as hell. Out of all my days ones, Murph was the jokester and a people person. No matter what walk of life you came from, Murph could walk up to you and have a full-fledged conversation.

Woop! Woop! Woop! A patrol car blue-lighted us. My first reaction was to mash the gas especially with the dope we had on the backseat, but I hadn't done shit, and all my papers for the Charger were legit. I closed the bags, and pulled over. Murph didn't say anything; he just gave me a look like if anything go wrong I had better get us out of there. If things went sour, I was confident the 600 horses I had under the hood would get me free. And I wasn't beyond letting a few shots off to ensure I got away.

"Man, we good," I said when I saw who the officer was.

"Is that Red Beard?"

I rolled down my window, as he walked up.

"Corrigan wants you, he said to cut the phone he gave you on," Red Beard said and walked off.

Murph handed me the flip phone out the glove compartment, and I cut it on. It instantly started ringing. I answered, and Corrigan told me to meet him at the Harris Teeter on Raeford Road.

"Don't you love when a plan comes together?" I asked Murph, and he grinned.

Corrigan didn't know it, but I wasn't content with him knowing so much about me, and me not knowing nothing about him. That was going to change today. I drove to the Harris Teeter, and parked beside Corrigan's black Suburban.

"What up?" I asked, getting in the SUV.

"A bag." Corrigan handed me another folder.

"Bet!" I hopped out, got in my Charger and peeled off. "Look, bra, you follow the young boy, and I'm going to follow Corrigan." I gave Murph the game plan as I tried to hurry up and get to the spot. After I came out of Karma's stash house, I stuck a tracking device inside the tire well of the G-wagon. I had pretty much figured the nigga wasn't going to tell us where Karma stayed, so this was my back up plan. Then before I got out of Corrigan's SUV, I discreetly dropped my iPhone inside the door panel. So I would be able to find him because my phone had a tracker in it. We got to the spot, put the bags of dope inside and swerved off, going in different directions.

The tracker led me back to the west side of the city, to an upscale housing area called Rayconda. Every house I passed looked to be at least a quarter million. I followed the dot on the tracker to a beige two-story building with a two-car garage, and green shutters. Corrigan's house—at least, I assumed it was his house—was rather modest, compared to all the others. I sped past because I didn't want to risk him seeing me. I drove out the housing area, and used the flip phone to call him.

"Yeah," he answered.

"I think I left my phone in your SUV."

"Hold on, let me check." I heard him walking and opening doors, then he said, "Yeah, I got it, where are you?"

"At the McDonalds in front of 71st High School."

"Give me ten minutes"

I hung up with Corrigan, and Murph called.

"Face, this nigga stay in the hood!"

"Who?"

"Karma, bro! He stay in them houses at the end of Ashton Road."

"Cut the bullshit."

"That's on God, my dog."

"Say no more, I'm gon' get up with you in a minute." I saw Corrigan's Suburban pull into McDonalds.

"You need to be more careful with your phone," he said, tossing me my phone.

I didn't respond. I was trying to formulate a plan on how to get at Karma. Corrigan was an afterthought now that I knew where he rested at. He only had one time to try and play me, and I was going to put his face in the obituaries.

Chapter Twenty

"Baby, why don't you do something with your money?" Cynthia asked me.

"I do. I spend it, and I spend it well." I slapped her on the butt of the Fendi onesie I had bought her.

"You do, baby." She smiled, sitting down in my lap. "But you can turn some of that illegal money into legit money."

"What illegal money? I'm a hardworking citizen. I'm employed by the city." This wasn't that far from the truth.

"Face, stop playing and listen." She grabbed my face with both of her hands.

"Before you start, Angel, let me go ahead and tell you. I don't want to hear shit about going legit because that's not in the cards for me. I was born a street nigga, and I'm gon' die a street nigga, so save your breath!" I let her know where I stood.

"Okay, Mr. Street Nigga, but what are you going to leave your child? Not a bunch of illegal money. I don't see a bunch of real street niggas that make it past twenty-one or even to twenty-one. Every day you're above ground is a blessing, and that shit keeps me up at night knowing you might die in the streets. And who would help me raise our baby?"

"This is what you signed up for when you agreed to be with me. Any time you feel like it's too much for you, let me know." I gave it to her raw. "And stop all of this baby talk. I ain't ready for all that."

"Well, why the hell do you be filling me up with your kids?" Cynthia mushed me in my head and stood up.

"You know my pull out game weak," I laughed.

"You laughing but I'm pregnant." She wiped the smile off my face. "Not smiling no more, huh?"

"Quit playing, Cynthia."

"I'm dead serious, Face, this isn't something I would play about."

I didn't need this right now. I had nothing against babies because I loved babies, especially when I could hand them off to their parents. I was no good for a child, not while I was still in the streets at least. I didn't want my baby to grow up without a father like I did. A child would fuck my mind state up. I wouldn't be able to just think about myself anymore. I would have to factor my kid into every decision I made, and that was a recipe for disaster in my line of work.

"You ain't got nothing to say?" Cynthia got in my face.

"Move, woman!" I was trying to wrap my mind around being a father.

"No! You act like you don't care!" She was starting to work herself up.

"Is it mine?"

Thwack! Cynthia slapped the fresh gum I was chewing out of my mouth.

"Don't you ever try to handle me like I'm a slut! I'm not one of them little young girls you're used to dealing with. I haven't even looked at another nigga since we became a couple." She jabbed me with her finger on every word that she spoke. "You act as if you want for me to have an abortion."

"If you kill my baby, I'm gon' kill you. When is your next doctor's appointment?"

"Next week, baby! I can't wait either." Her whole mood had changed upon hearing that I didn't want her to abort my baby. "Oh and we're going to my parents' house for Christmas."

"Why you always bossing me around?"

"'Cause I'm a boss bitch!" Cynthia shot back. "Matter of fact, grab your keys, we about to go out." She ran in the back.

"I don't feel like going anywhere, today is my day to relax!" I yelled.

"You can relax when we get there!" She yelled from the back of her apartment. "You'll thank me later!"

I laid on the couch, got comfortable and thought of what it was going to be like to have a baby. Aw, man, my mom was going to flip out when I told her.

"Face, get up"

"Where you think you going with that little, tight ass dress on?" Cynthia had changed into a grey Chanel mini that had a white Chanel belt made into it.

"You mean where *we* going?—And you the one who bought it," she said, doing a little pirouette, showing me her body. "Let's go." Cynthia pulled me up, and started pushing me towards the door.

We got outside, and into my Audi, with her driving. Cynthia reached into her Chanel purse, and tossed a bundle of money in my lap.

"Take that in."

"In where?" I thumbed through the blue and purple faced bills. There was about twenty thousand. "And where you get this bread from?"

"You're not the only one with money," Cynthia bragged.

I got my question of where we were going answered when she pulled over into *Secrets*, a strip club on Bragg Boulevard. I had never been to a strip club before. I didn't understand how dudes threw their hard-earned money at naked women who, if they'd seen them in the mall, probably wouldn't even get a *hey, how you doing?*

Tricking was not in my blood, and I had it. I respected strippers though. I respected every body's hustle, and that's what I felt like was happening when niggas threw money. I just wasn't in the business of getting hustled. We walked inside of the strip club, and my head started spinning. I loved bad bitches, and every way I turned there was a half-naked chick walking by. But I still didn't have the urge to throw no bread. "Baby, go to the counter and trade the money for some ones, I'm going to go get us a VIP spot." Cynthia sashayed away.

Normally, I would watch her walk away, but I had my eyes on all the naked women that kept walking by.

"I'm trying to get some ones," I told the pretty chick sitting behind the counter.

"How much?"

"Twenty-two," I said, reaching into my pockets.

"Twenty-two dollars! Boy, you need to stop." She covered her mouth, laughing.

"Thousand." I put the money on the counter, and her eyes about popped out of her head.

I smirked, as she put her head down and began counting the money. I watched as she stood up and bent over to grab some ones, allowing the dress that she had on to ride up and show me that she wasn't wearing any panties.

"My bad," she said, handing me the stack of singles.

"That shit ain't about nothing, you good." I grabbed the money, and walked in the VIP section.

Cynthia was drinking some water when I got in VIP. I sat the money on the table, and sat down beside my bitch.

"What are you having?" I rubbed on her stomach.

"You mean what are we having?" She placed her hand on top of mine.

"You know what I mean."

"It's too early to find out. What do you want?"

"A boy."

"Anyways—" She rolled her eyes.

"You want a dance, boo?" an Indian-looking stripper with silky black hair down to her ass asked me.

"Nah, I'm good."

"Yes, he do, go ahead and do your thing," Cynthia told her and grabbed some ones.

I watched as the stripper started moving what body she did have. She was, maybe, 5'6, about 130 pounds, had a mouthful of titties, and a little tootie booty. Her pecan- colored skin was littered with glitter. What she lacked in the body department she made up for it with her looks. She looked like Pocahontas. She bent over, showing me her fat pussy, and Cynthia started throwing ones on her. Seeing my bitch was into it, I slapped the stripper on the ass. She got in my lap and started grinding her hips, looking me in my eyes. She leaned up, and put her A-cups in my face. That was too much temptation. I forgot all about Cynthia being beside me because I took one of the stripper's breasts into my mouth. She grabbed the back of my head, pulling me closer to her.

"A'ight now, bitch!" Cynthia said, and I leaned back.

"Shut up, Cynthia."

The stripper laughed.

"Move off of my baby, Pocahontas." Cynthia pushed her.

"Y'all know each other?" I was confused.

"Yes, boo, we do," said Cynthia.

Cynthia stared lustfully at me with steamy eyes, nibbling on the tip of one of her manicured nails. She was obviously aroused from watching me and the stripper girl. "Boo, this is my girlfriend."

"Girlfriend?" I broke in incredulously.

Cynthia shook her head, playfully mushed me, and corrected. "Girlfriend, as in *best*, fool."

We all shared a chuckle. Then Cynthia continued her formal introduction by snuggling to me and identifying me as: 'Face, her baby's daddy'.

"Baby daddy?" Pocahontas said, and looked at her, not fully understanding.

"I'm pregnant, bitch!" Cynthia beamed.

"That's why yo' ass drinking water. He look like a little young boy, let me find out you robbing cradles now," she smiled.

I hadn't said anything. I was watching them go back and forth.

"My baby is seventeen, he turn eighteen next month. He carries himself better than half the niggas in here, and his stroke game the best I ever had." Cynthia bragged.

"Is that right?" Pocahontas looked in my lap.

"Mind how you stare, he off limits, but I might give him a treat for his birthday. It depends on how he act. This his first time coming to a strip club, too. But that's not the reason I brought him here. He's thinking about opening a strip club, and I wanted to show him how much money he could make and how easy it is." This thing Cynthia just told her girlfriend was something I knew nothing about.

"You need to because I'm tired of this place, and I can bring twenty bad bitches with me," Pocahontas said.

"Tell him how much money the club makes on a good week," Cynthia said.

"No less than thirty thousand."

I did the math in my head. That was a hundred and twenty thousand a month, and one point four million a year. Cynthia might be onto something.

"I told you, bae, and you ain't got to do shit but hire someone to run it, which would be me," said Cynthia.

"What you know about running a strip club?" I asked.

"Oh, he don't know?" asked Pocahontas.
"Know what?" I asked.
"That's how we met. I used to work here."

Nicholas Lock

Chapter Twenty-One

When me and Murph finally got around to counting the bricks of heroin we had hit Karma for, we counted up sixty-five of them. That was going to lace our pockets with about nine hundred thousand apiece once we got all of them sold. It wouldn't take long because we were selling them for thirty a pop; niggas was gonna love that. I was more than likely just gon' front my half to Ross, and let him do his thing. I definitely wasn't going to allow them to be around me.

"Bra, who did Corrigan have in the folder?" Murph asked, rolling up a blunt.

In all honesty, I had been so caught up in the fast life that I had forgotten all about the folder. Curious of the contents that it held, I went to go retrieve it. Before I returned to the living room, I had the folder open.

"Work," I tossed the name and face around in my memory bank.

I did not know the nigga.

"You know this nigga Work?" I continued to flip through the folder.

"He got robbed yesterday, and they shot him in the ass— And I heard he got hit for eighty thousand, and twenty pounds of gas—I don't know who robbing these niggas but the nigga not playing no games," Murph said, passing me the blunt.

"That's a fact. In the last two months I've heard of at least ten niggas that this nigga done hit. He stupid though because he always shoot them in the ass. That's like his calling card or something; it lets everyone know it was him." I took two hits of the weed, and instantly relaxed.

I texted Corrigan and told him somebody beat me to the punch. He texted me back, and said he already knew but he would have something else for us in a little bit.

"Bro, that nigga Karma is far from a dummy. I be driving to the back of the hood where he stay, scoping shit out, right? I tried driving down the street he stay on, and could only get half way down the block before niggas blocked the street off and told me I had to turn around. I wasn't trying to make a scene, so I turned around. You know I wasn't going for that, so the next day I put my football gear on and jogged down his street—"

"Wait, wait, wait. Your big ass was jogging?" I cracked up laughing.

"Okay, I wasn't jogging. I was doing a slow trot but anyway they let me go by, but they watched me the whole time. The street he stay on is a big P, and every house from the halfway point and all the way around the curve are his team. That's why they wouldn't let me drive through because they knew it was no reason for me to be there. And that nigga Karma house is huge! It looked like he tore down two houses and built one big one." Murph gave me the rundown.

I had my eyes closed, feeling the effects of the gas we were passing back and forth, but I was formulating a plan as to how to get at Karma. There was always a weak link. I just had to figure it out. It was obvious we couldn't go through the front, but what about the back?

"Murph, what's behind the house?"

"I don't know the name of the street, but it's the side street off Cumberland Road beside the building that Congo use to be in."

"Fuck it. Tonight we gon' see what that shit hitting on, and if it's an opening, we can take it. Even if we can't rob him, he needs to be dealt with because if it get out that we killed Lucky, niggas gon' try to do us in for that bounty."

"Say less. I'm gon' catch up to you later—I got to meet Vanessa at the doctor," Murph said.

"The doctor?"

"She pregnant." He grinned. "We both about to be daddies." He reminded me that Cynthia was pregnant.

I had kind've warmed to the idea of having a mini me running around. Me and Murph left the house together. I had to get some things in order before tonight. I was pulling into Sandpipers to get me some shrimp and hush puppies when an unfamiliar number called my phone.

"Yo?" I answered.

"Nymel?" a female questioned coyly.

"Laci."

"Oh what's happening, buddy?"

"Me getting pampered. What happened to that?"

Suddenly it hit me like a ton of bricks. I had forgotten all about my end of the bargain. I mean if it was not for Laci, then I would have never hit for all those bricks of heroin in the first place.

The least I could do was cover the small price it took to pay to get her hair and nails done up.

"You ready right now?" I asked.

"I am. I stay in the new apartments in Grove View Terrace all the way in the back."

"I'm right here at Sandpipers, so I'll be there in about three minutes."

I got my food, and drove down the road to Laci's apartment. Damn! I hadn't been through since they had remodeled the projects. It was still hood though, because there were bitches hanging out their window talking to one another as if phones weren't a thing. I drove around to the back and saw a group of bad bitches shooting dice. When they saw the Audi, they stopped the dice, trying to see who was driving, but the tint kept that from happening.

"Where you at, girl?" I called Laci

"I spilled something on my pants, so I'm about to change, just come on in."

"Which one you stay in?"

"Here I come."

I was about to tell her no, but she had already hung up. I took a deep breath, grabbed my Glock 20, and got out. "Who you here for?" one of the girls questioned.

"Laci."

"No way," another said.

"You like 'em big, don't you?" said another one.

"You can do better than that," a thick redbone said.

I was about to respond, but I saw Laci waving me over. I strolled over to Laci, and followed her inside her apartment. The shit was nice and clean, it had a cosy feel to it. I sat down on the green leather couch, and grabbed the remote.

"Damn, nigga! You just made yourself right at home, didn't you?" Laci grinned.

"Hurry up and change, girl, so we can go."

I could hear Laci notably smack her lips. When I turned to face her, she was standing there with her hands on her hips.

"Come to think of it, don't you owe me a massage as well?"

Laci was being fast.

"Girl, go in, get your shit together, and we gon' get all that taken care of at the massage parlor." I shifted my attention to the television, and turned to ESPN.

Laci did not respond just then. There was a distinguished silence. I could feel Laci's eyes on me, watching me. Only once she saw that she had my attention did she, in a steamy and sinful breath, say: "Face—" That erotic heartbeat of silence returned. "Face, I don't just want anybody's hands on my body." As if losing herself, her hands had gravitated to her large bosom, caressing them, and enticingly fondling their sensitive tips through the fabric of her shirt. "Face, I need yours."

Despite my efforts to stay focused on the mission at hand, I could feel myself getting caught up.

Laci's eyes shifted to my crotch area. Her eyes widened a bit, as she and I watched the awakening of my manhood, pulsing, rising to tent the front of my Champion sweats.

I felt my dick throb with a burst of joy to see Laci nibbling demurely on the tip of one of her nails. There was a seductive glint in her eyes that let me know that she wanted to fuck.

I nodded to the spot on the couch beside me.

"I want to be able to lay down and relax, come—" Laci grabbed hold of one of my hands with a bit more urgency than I'm sure she did not mean for me to see.

She was leading me on with a sexy sashay. My eyes had been drawn to the sight of her booty. The erotic and seductive motion of her hips.

When we entered the bedroom, I pushed Laci on top of the mattress. Her sinful nature was contagious, and I found myself commanding her to strip!

Laci, weak with lust, complied.

When she got down to her panties and bra, suddenly, she became a good girl; our roles were reversed, and it was me unclasping her bra.

The sight of her big beautiful breasts springing out made my dick surge with a powerful rush of sexual adrenaline. I went for her panties.

Laci bashfully sealed her legs. "Face, I'm not one of these little hoes that you are used to dealing with," she whispered weakly, and as if for the record, she added; "Out of my entire twenty years of living, I only had sex with one person."

The mood changed. Laci innocently reminded me that I was only in her bedroom so that I could uphold my end of the bargain with her massage.

I collected myself enough to delicately lay her on her belly, and began massaging her back.

"So—" Laci released a simmering breath, "Whatever happened to you and that girl Rai'chell?" she asked, slipping into a deep comfortable state. "Y'all made a pretty couple."

Hearing Rai'chell's name made me tense up. I removed my hands from her body.

She got the point, apologized, and spun around to face me on her back. She was wearing a little sad puppy face, and with her eyes she was pleading for me not to end the luxurious feeling of her massage.

In all truth, I was fiending. Laci's innocent-shy girl nature had me on the wire!

My hands went up to her shoulders. Mischievously, I pressed my groin against her crotch. My eyes were lustfully appraising her voluptuous breasts.

The soft sounds of her pleasures were both heartfelt and stimulating. Laci kept demanding, "Lower—Low—Lower" Somehow, I ended up with the bulging print of my manhood grazing against her face as my hands slipped inside of her panties.

She was soaked! My hand rubbed her clit, fingered her sex. "Why you been trying me?" I reached into my joggers, and came out with my johnson. I smacked each of her cheeks with it, and glossed her sexy lips with my arousal. "Now I'ma make you suck on this dick until it bust."

"You not the boss of me. You can't make me do anything that I don't want to do."

With that said, she opened her mouth to reveal her tongue ring, and slurped me in. She took her time, looking me up into the eyes the entire time.

She hastily got out of the bed, fell to her knees before me, and proceeded to worship me as if I were a god. She was taking me to the back of her throat, holding me there, then letting me come out of her mouth until the tip of me was encased by her luscious lips. As she twirled her tongue ring around the head as if it were a lollipop, she privileged me with the sight of her fingering her love box deep, long, fast, slow and all in a provocative manner.

Suddenly, I felt my nut simmering, boiling, and instinctively I seized a fistful of hair. I was fucking her mouth, slutting her out in. Before long, I was erupting. I thought Laci was going to try and spit out, but she swallowed me all up like a good girl, and kept right on sucking!

"Ho! Ho!" I withdrew my pole from her mouth.

"Oh, so you running, huh?"

Admitting defeat and feeling weak, I pulled up my sweats. "You got that off."

In a feline manner Laci rolled over to her back on the carpet floor. And to my surprise, she demonstrated her flexibility by pulling a single leg back to her ear. She was lightly caressing her twat, while staring dreamily into my eyes.

"If you think the head game popping, then wait until you try this." Full of temptations, she inserted her fingers, sliding them in slow, deep!

Laci had a pretty pussy.

I found myself between her chubby thick thighs. My eyes took in the sight of her. Laci had a pretty face, she wasn't sloppy fat but simply big-boned, and her figure was deeply defined by her curves.

Never before had I seen a big girl who could hold her weight so well.

In a lusting and faraway state, I had begun to unconsciously slide the thick bulbous head of my manhood between her thick vaginal lips. I was coating her crotch with her glistening love.

Suddenly, my mind was jerked to Cynthia, her popping up pregnant, and babies. "You got any condoms, Laci?"

"Nymel—" Laci sang my name in a way that tugged at my common sense. "Nymel, I told you I only had sex with one person my entire life. And that was back two years ago when we were still in school."

Laci confessed innocently.

I lost all resistance when she seized a strong hold on my dick and guided me inside of her.

I was no more good. She was soaked, gripping like pliers, and I fell deep into her in one slick, bone-gliding motion.

Laci moaned.

I groaned.

We began to groove. My mouth was lovely devouring one of her thick nipples, pushing back further on the leg elevated behind her head.

We were a wild entanglement on the floor. Laci, wanting to put on for the big girls, found her way on top of me. She was surprisingly light, and skilled. "I been wanting to do this ever since I saw your little young ass your freshman year," revealed Laci, as she passionately surfed on my cock.

I was on the verge of busting. Reflexively, I felt my toes curl. I grabbed, palmed, and spread her cheeks far and wide.

As if she could see me holding on by a thread, she smirked down on me, and deviously began to flex her walls. "This pussy too good for your little young ass."

That was it. I couldn't take anymore, and I exploded inside of her. Laci threw her head back. I could feel my stick of joy pulsing ecstatically inside of her, and triggering her to orgasm.

Nicholas Lock

Chapter Twenty-Two

Me and Murph pulled up to our duck off spot at the same time.
"Damn, nigga, why you look so tired?" Murph asked me.
"You don't want to know."

I walked inside the house, went straight to my room, and
grabbed a hammer. Laci's pussy was so fiyah that I had left
my Glock at her house.

I walked back out into the living room, and Murph was
sitting on the love seat, loading slugs into a pistol grip Mossberg. I pushed everything to the back of my mind. It was time
to put in work, and I didn't need any distractions. We didn't
have a rental, so we were going to drive my Escalade. I definitely wasn't going to drive my Audi, and Cynthia had my
Charger. I turned Kevin Gates' single—"Walls Talking"—all
the way up, and drove off. We were both quiet while we rode
to our side of town. Me and Murph knew each other so well;
no words were needed. I cut the radio down when I turned
onto Cumberland Road. I turned down the side street beside
Congo's, and parked at one of the empty apartments on the
street. We got out, and walked behind the apartment, and into
the woods that sat behind them. It was eerily quiet except for
a few crickets chirping, and leaves crunching under our feet.
We only had to walk through the woods a few minutes before
we got to the back of Karma's house, which was enclosed in
a 10-foot tall privacy fence.

Karma's house was huge; it stood out among all the other
houses. His house wasn't a two-story, but what it lacked in
height it made up for in length. There had to at least be six
bedrooms; I could tell that by looking at the back of the house.
I wasn't concerned about the layout of the house. I needed to
find a flaw or a way to get inside without being detected. I
looked at the steam rising off the water, letting me know the

pool was heated. I didn't understand how Karma had been living right under our noses, and we didn't know it.

"My hands are freezing." Murph put the Mossberg under his arm, and blew into his hands, while I climbed up the privacy fence.

"It's definitely cold as a bitch," I added, peeking over the wooden fence.

I continued to check Karma's house out. I didn't see any cameras or anything out of the ordinary that caught my attention. I knew it was a long shot that I would actually have a chance to get at Karma on a whim, but I had to give it a try.

A light came on in the kitchen, and two bad bitches ran out naked and jumped in the pool. Two minutes later, Karma appeared in the backdoor, watching the two chicks splash each other. While Lucky had been husky and tall, Karma was skinny as hell, and short, with two braids going to the back.

"Come on, Karma, come swim with us," one of the girls said.

"I'm good where I'm at," Karma said from the doorway.

"Murph, if this nigga get his ass in that pool, I'm hopping this fence," I whispered.

"And I'm gon' be right behind you," he said.

"Karma, if you don't get in with us we not fucking," the other chick said.

Karma thought it over for a second, then took his clothes off, and hopped in the pool. He was still in the air when I hopped the wooden fence. When he broke the surface of the water, I put the gun in his face, causing the girls to scream.

"Scream again, and I'll turn this pool red," I said.

"Watch them," I told Murph when he walked up beside me.

"You're making a deadly mistake," Karma said, but I ignored him.

I went in the house to make sure they were alone. Once satisfied, I locked the doors and walked back outside.

"Come on," I motioned with the gun for them to get out the pool.

"If you make so much as a peep, I'm gon' splatter your brains on the floor," Murph said.

We got them inside, and sat them down on the couch in the massive living room. I sat across from Karma on a leather sofa.

"Now, Karma, I'm more than sure you know what this shit is hitting for, so let's cut out all the bullshit and get to it. I want that three million dollar bounty you put on us."

"You're the one that killed my brother! Fuck you, pussy! I ain't giving you country niggas a dime!"

Normally, I would have applauded his bravado but his wasn't authentic because he wasn't tied up; so if he really wanted to buck, there wasn't a thing stopping him.

"Karma, cut the shenanigans!" I laughed. "You're gonna give us what we came for, one way or the other. Which way is up to you." I leaned back and crossed my arms.

"The deep freezer is a safe!" one of the girls blurted out.

"Lauren, I'm gon' kill your bird ass!" Karma growled.

"Fuck you, nigga! You treat me like shit anyway. Got me fucking my little sister and shit. Driving your work on the interstate. You treat me like a mule when I'm supposed to be your lady!" She fumed.

I looked at the two chicks and, sure enough, they favored each other. It didn't surprise me, though. Money made people do strange things.

"If I had a gun, I would kill you myself, nigga!" Lauren snapped.

I walked to the kitchen, and left Murph with the bickering couple. I lifted the lid on the deep freezer, and all I saw were different kinds of meats.

"Yo, Lauren, bring your lying ass here!" I yelled.

She came in the kitchen with a scared look on her face.

"Ain't shit but meat in there." I was about to put her thinking cap all over the kitchen.

She walked over to the deep freezer, and bent over inside the deep freezer. We hadn't allowed them to put their clothes back on; so when she bent over, her pussy smiled at me. Lauren was an Amazon! She was at least 5'11 and about a hundred and eighty pounds. She had an even, mocha complexion. Her eyes were chinky with long, naturally curly eyelashes. Her breasts were double D's, and her ass was out of this world. Every little move she made, her ass would jiggle for about three seconds. I grabbed a handful of her ass to see how soft it was, and she stiffened up.

"You good, ma, I'm not in the business of taking pussy— I'll take anything but that," I said, and she looked back at me, and smirked, then went back to whatever it was she was doing.

Her ass was stupid soft! It was a shame her gorgeous ass had to die, but that was the price she had to pay for fucking with a street nigga. Lauren stood up with the meat from the freezer on a rack that I had missed. I looked in the freezer and saw the door of the safe, so she hadn't been lying. I didn't see a keypad, though.

"Karma has to put his hand on it for it to open," she said.

This nigga Karma had some exclusive shit! Oh yea, this was going to be a hell of a payday for us. I made Lauren walk ahead of me, going back to the living room.

"I need to borrow your hand Karma," I told him.

"Can y'all let us go? We don't have anything to do with this," Lauren's sister pleaded.

"Karla, shut up! You think they're going to let y'all bitches leave? Ha! They don't have masks on, the only people leaving this house alive is them, dummy!" Karma spoke the absolute truth.

"Don't call my sister no dummy! You're the reason we're even in this situation!" Lauren charged him.

Karma and Lauren started fighting, making Murph yell: "Sit the fuck down!"

Then Karma produced a chrome .380 out of nowhere, and wrapped his arm around Lauren's neck, using her as a shield.

"You boys fucked up," Karma grinned, and backed up towards the front door.

He couldn't have been thinking straight because we didn't give two fucks about her. I was about to shoot him and her when Karla, who was also an Amazon, rushed Karma.

"Get off my sister!" She peppered him with punches. Lauren got loose, and grabbed the hand Karma had the gun in, while Karla grabbed his wood and twisted. Murph tucked his gun, and tried to break them up while I had my fire trained on them all. Karma let go of the gun, relinquishing it to Lauren. She put the gun to his head, and let off a single shot, blowing the back of Karma's head out. Then Lauren turned, and put the gun to Murph's head. I don't know why in the fuck he had gotten so close in the first place.

I saw a look in Lauren's eyes that I assumed was the look I had in my eyes when I had killed DJ.

"Put the gun down, Lauren," I said.

"Why? So you can kill me?" She moved her sister behind her as if to protect her.

"Look, I'm not gon' kill you, but you have to get your hands dirty for me. You said Karma was doing you dirty so here's your chance to do him dirty." I tried reasoning with her.

I knew without a doubt that I could kill her, but I didn't want her to pull the trigger reflexively and kill Murph. He'd gotten lucky the first time he had gotten shot, but he wouldn't survive a bullet at point-blank range.

"What you mean?" Lauren asked.

"We can talk about it, but you have to give my nigga the gun first," I said, getting ready to squeeze.

She looked me in the eyes for ten seconds straight, as if trying to read me, and handed Murph the gun. *Thwack!*

He slapped her to her knees, and put the gun to her head.

"Chill, bro, I got her," I said.

"Lauren, we have to get in the safe. I need you to cut Karma's hand off." I was trying to see if she really had that killer instinct.

Murph went in the kitchen, came back out, and tossed a butcher knife at her feet. He made sure not to get too close this time, and I laughed in my head. I was definitely gon' roast his ass later on.

Lauren wiped the blood out the corner of her mouth with the back of her hand. She picked the knife up slowly, as if she was deciding whether or not to do it, then brought the butcher knife down on Karma's wrist. Lauren started hacking away at Karma's wrist. Every time she brought the knife up, blood would splatter on her face. She was so out of it she didn't bother to wipe it off. Lauren cut through to the bone then snapped Karma's hand off, and tossed it at my feet.

I looked at Murph, and said: "Oh, bitch! She was gon' kill you."

I grabbed the hand, and went to go open the safe. I had no idea what I was doing.

"Like this—" Lauren had snuck up on me, but Murph was right there.

She slid a metal flap over, revealing a hand-shaped sensor. Lauren placed Karma's hand on the sensor, and the safe started hissing, then the safe door popped. I flipped the safe door up, and was sorely disappointed. The safe was lined with money, but I could tell it wasn't close to what we had hit Lucky for.

"Come here, Lauren," I said. She and her sister had huddled together by the sink. "By law I'm supposed to kill both of you, but I'm giving you a pass. That money yours, you earned it. If I see my face on the news, I'm going to hunt you down and make you watch as I skin your sister alive."

"Bro, you tripping" Murph said.

"Nah, I got a good feeling about them. Let's bounce."

"Wait till I tell Trip about this tender dick ass shit you doing. Letting the hoes keep the money." Murph mumbled.

He reached in the safe, grabbed a bundle of money, and walked out the backdoor. I looked at Lauren and her sister one last time before I left. I hoped like hell my decision didn't come back to haunt me.

Nicholas Lock

Chapter Twenty-Three

"So what exactly is it that you do?" Cynthia's dad asked curiously.

Cynthia had taken me to her parents' house to have Sunday dinner. They stayed deep in the country and far across the river in a massive Victorian two-story house. Their closest neighbor was a football field away. I could tell her dad did not approve of me, but her mom wouldn't let me go. She had latched onto me. My assumptions were right. I knew that Cynthia was mixed with something, I didn't know exactly what until this moment.

Now here before me were her parents—A middle-aged white guy, and a pretty peanut butter brown doll for a mother.

"Billy, I wish you would leave this young man alone." Her mother defended me.

"It's okay, Ms. Weeks."

"Call me Courtney, hon. *Ms. Weeks* makes me feel old. Besides, you're a part of the family now that you and our baby girl are having a baby."

I smiled, and turned to her dad. "I'm actually in the process of starting my own business with your daughter. Once that gets up and running, I plan on starting my own talent agency. I played high school football at a high level, so I have a good eye for talent." *What a lie!* I thought

"What school did you play for?" asked her father with a skeptical look that was breaking down with every passing moment. Then, suddenly, his eyes lit up with recognition. "Wait, wait a minute, you have a twin, right?" he asked, and I nodded. "I graduated from Douglas Byrd myself. I've been following you and your brother since you guys were freshmen. Why didn't you go on to college like your brother? You were rated as the number one linebacker in the country. You would've been playing on Sundays soon."

Cynthia's dad surprised me with his knowledge about me. "I fell out of love with the game."

"Dad, you sound like a groupie," Cynthia chimed in with a face of mockery.

He shooed her along distractedly with his hand. "Hush up, Cynthia." Then, shifting his attention to me, he instructed: "Come on, son, let me show you something" He pushed himself up from the table.

Cynthia tried to get up and follow us, but he obstructed her path, and told her to stay along with her mother. He led me upstairs to his man cave. There was Douglas Byrd High, UNC, and Carolina Panther paraphernalia everywhere. He passed me on Icehouse, and motioned for me to sit down.

"Nymel, I'm going to be straight with you. That's my only child out there, and I'll move mountains to see her happy and safe."

I nodded in agreement "As would I, Mr. Weeks."

A silent promise was made. And with the covenant between us, I earned a smile of approval from the old man.

"She's only brought one other boyfriend to meet us, and that was in high school. Her bringing you here let me know she really likes you. It's your job to keep her happy and safe, and it's a job I'm holding you to. I don't care the circumstance or what you have to do to do it."

"Cynthia is going to be my wife one day, so her well-being and happiness is my top priority."

We clinked beers, and he turned on the football game. The Panthers were playing the Atlanta Falcons. If they beat the Falcons, they would be in the playoffs. At halftime our women came in, and sat in our laps.

"What did he want?" Cynthia whispered in my ear.

"Nothing serious." I wasn't going to tell her.

"Dad, what have y'all been talking about?"

"Men stuff," he responded, his eyes never leaving the game.

Cynthia huffed, folded her arms and leaned back in my lap. Cynthia was so spoiled and used to having her way that if she didn't, she would pout. I ignored the mini tantrum she was throwing, and watched the game.

"I'm ready to go." Cynthia stood up. "Bye, ma—bye, dad," she said, and walked out.

I said my goodbyes, and left to go deal with Cynthia's bratty ass. Some good sex and the promise of getting her the new Birkin clutch ended her bad mood.

Our birthday was next week, and I had to make sure Trip was going to show up. He had gone to college and fell in love with college life, then he had UNC playing for the National Championship for the first time in school history, and he had won the Heisman trophy. Mel Kiper Jr. and Todd McShay were already pegging Trip as the number one draft pick when he came out. I pulled up to his apartment, and knocked on the door. A foreign chick answered the door in a t-shirt that barely covered her treasure chest.

"Tymel, I thought you weren't going to be back until tonight." She let me in and closed the door.

It was clear from her statement that she thought I was Trip. She must've been the girl he had told me about. She was from India, and loved to suck dick but wouldn't give him no pussy. Trip told me she was just his slut. So he wasn't going to mind if I tested the goodies out. I didn't respond; instead, I walked in the kitchen to get me something to drink.

"I know you hear me." She walked up behind me.

I grabbed a Gatorade, and turned around. She got in my face and repeated: "I know you hear me." I put the Gatorade on the counter, put my hands on her shoulders, and pushed her onto her knees. She was definitely a slut because she grabbed my jeans and pulled my dick out. She didn't waste any time taking me into her mouth. Her head game was mediocre, I wasn't impressed. I looked up, and saw Trip come in; she had her back to the door, so she couldn't see him. He saw me and smiled, then motioned to the couch, and raised his hand up and down. He was trying to train her, something we had done to numerous chicks. Trip went in the back, and I got her to the couch. I laid back on the couch, and she bent over and put my wood back in her mouth. Trip came out, and got behind her. He grabbed her by her hips, and her eyes got big. She turned and saw Trip standing behind her, then looked back at me.

"Oh my God!" She shrieked. "Which one of you is Tymel?" she asked, but I knew that she was with the game plan because she still had my pole in her hands.

"Me, Lydia," said Trip, causing her to look back at me.

She narrowed her eyes and said, "You tricked me"

I grinned, and guided her head back to where it belonged. She welcomed me back with a wide open mouth. Tripped flipped her t-shirt up, and started pounding her out. We trained her for about thirty minutes straight, it ended with Trip busting in her mouth. I pulled out of her, and busted all over her face.

"Just like old times," I said, as Lydia went to clean up.

"Hell yeah." Trip laughed.

"You know we having a birthday bash at Club *Diamonds,*" I said.

"I ain't gon' be able to make it. We can celebrate again"

This would be the first time we wouldn't be together for our birthday. Lydia came out the back, and sat down between us.

"You guys better not tell nobody what we did," she warned. Me and my twin started laughing.

"Your secret's safe with us," I said.

"It better be," she said. "Now who's first?"

"First what?" asked Trip.

"In my mouth."

Me and Trip looked at each other and smiled. I could see why he loved college so much.

Nicholas Lock

Chapter Twenty-Four

My birthday started off great! I woke up to Cynthia's mouth licking up and down my shaft, then she rode me until we both climaxed. Subsequently, we went to the doctor's office, and found out we were having a girl.

"I got another surprise for you, baby." Cynthia smiled

"What?"

"I'm about to show you."

We were riding in Cynthia's Lexus because she had insisted on driving. I was sitting in the passenger seat, staring at her.

"Why are you staring at me?"

"'Cause you're beautiful."

"Aww!" Cynthia leaned over, and gave me a kiss so sensual my little man rocked up.

Cynthia was looking so good it was crazy. The pregnancy had her skin glowing. Cynthia was already thick, but she was getting thicker; she had gone up two sizes in jeans. And her breasts went from 34 C's to 34 D's. The baby was totally reshaping her body, and I loved it. I reached over, and lifted the Alexander McQueen blouse she had on, and rubbed her stomach. Cynthia put her hand on top of mine, and said: "I love you."

"Love you more." I slid my hand lower, into the waistband of her Alexander McQueen slacks, and rubbed on her clit through the panties she had on.

"We're here." She moved my hand.

I looked up, and saw we were on my side of town at the shopping center off Raeford Road beside Oakdale.

"What are we doing here?"

"Come on, and I'll show you."

We got out, and she led me up to the empty building towards the back of the shopping center. Before I could ask her what the hell she had going on, Cynthia produced a set of keys, and opened the doors to the building.

"Surprise!" she yelled. "This is the building for your strip club."

I had really forgotten about the whole idea. I was focused on getting rich, not starting no strip club. I looked around the empty building, trying to envision it being a strip club, and came up empty.

"You don't like it," she said, seeing the look on my face. "Come here, bae. Look, that's where the bar is going to be, the main stage will be there, there will be three VIP rooms." She tried explaining it, but I really wasn't interested.

"Just tell me how much it's gon' cost, and I'll get it to you." The club was going to be hers more than anything.

"Whatever, Nymel!" Cynthia stormed out the building.

I ran and caught up to her, and spun her around. She was crying, something she was doing a lot of lately. The pregnancy had her hormones all over the place.

"Get off of me! I went through hell getting that building, and you act so nonchalant about it. Don't you see I'm doing this for you? For our daughter! So her father can have some legal money and get out the streets! I don't want to be a single mother, and I don't want to have to bring your daughter to see you in prison!" She cried into my chest.

"Calm down, Angel. It's not that I don't care, it's just—I don't know, baby. But if it means that much to you, I'm going to become a little more invested in it. I love you, bae. Now chill out before you stress my daughter out. Then I'm gon' have to fuck you up." I picked her up, carried her over to the car, and sat her on the trunk.

"Move," Cynthia put her head in my chest, trying to hide her smile.

"So this is where my bitch been!" a voice said from behind me.

I turned to see Rude Boy sitting in a red BMW 4 series with a Mac10 in his hand. *Damn! I was about to get smoked on my eighteenth birthday.*

"You ain't so tough without your gun, huh?" Rude Boy grinned.

"I'm a gangsta, nigga! So fuck you two times!" If I was gon' die it wasn't going to be like no bitch.

"Jerome, leave us alone." Cynthia tried to get up, but I kept her behind me.

"Bitch, shut up! You know you'll be back to my house sooner or later, you always find your way back. And you, little nigga. I got your life in my hands. You think because I ain't struck yet that I'm not? You can't outthink me, little boy, but I need you to hurt before you die." With that, he rode off.

I was steaming hot! I hated to be caught lacking, and it was Cynthia's fault because she had made me leave my gun at home. Then the fact that he had spared my life didn't sit well with me. He had something up his sleeve, and I didn't plan on finding out what it was.

After my run in with Rude Boy, I got my gun and dropped Cynthia's ass off at her house. I went by Angie's, got some more birthday sex, and rode out. I had to get my hair cut. I got a text, as I parked in the parking lot. I looked and saw Rai'chell had sent me a birthday cake picture saying *Happy Birthday*. I started to text her back, but didn't. I still had love for her and if I opened that line of communication up, it was a good chance I would be going to her house.

"Birthday boy!" my barber—T-Mack—said when I walked in.

"We was just talking about Trip," Mr. C, the old-school barber of the shop, said.

Mr. C was 77, and could still cut with the best of them, and was in excellent shape. Every day after he got off, he went to the gym, and played ball or hit the weights. He was about 6'2, slim, brown-skinned, with grey littering his fade and beard.

"What about him?" I took my seat in T-Mack's chair.

"How he about to smoke Alabama's weak secondary and win UNC their first football championship," Mr. C said.

"I don't know—This might be Alabama's best defense," a dude waiting for a haircut said, setting Mr. C off.

T-Mack cut my hair while I listened to Mr. C give dude all the reasons why UNC was going to win.

"And if this knucklehead would've gone and played middle linebacker, UNC would've been unstoppable," he said.

T-Mack was finishing my hair, and I was glad I knew Mr. C was about to get on my case, but I didn't have time for it.

"Face, you need to take that scholarship and go to the NFL, "Mr. C said.

A lot of people didn't know it but UNC had offered me a scholarship too; nonetheless, I was done with school.

"I did take it, just not to UNC. I'm fully enrolled in the *University of the Streets*." I gave T-Mack his tip, and started walking towards the door.

"I heard of that school but I bet you didn't know that their graduation rate is zero percent—Nobody graduates, they either drop out or get kicked out," he said to my back.

I walked out, letting his words hang in the air. I was pulling my jeans up to get in the Audi when someone said, "Yo, Face."

I turned to see a tall high yellow nigga with French braids standing off to the side of me, wearing a mean mug. I tried to get my hammer off my hip, but it was too late. The dude had a cannon in his hand. I was standing on the inside of my door, so I couldn't run without giving him my back.

His first three shots found home, knocking me inside the car. I reached for my pistol again, and he hit me two more times, knocking the breath from my body. It felt like my chest was on fire! He walked up to the car with his gun dangling at his side. My mind said to fight, but my body wouldn't move. I looked him in the face, but didn't recognize him. He pulled his gun up, put it in my face and pulled the trigger.

Click! Click! His gun had jammed. *Boom! Boom! Boom!* The window of my car door shattered, making the dude duck and take off running. T-Mack and Mr. C ran up with guns in their hands.

"Call the ambulance!" T-Mack yelled. "Relax, Face you gon' be good."

I tried to say something, but only coughed up blood. It was over for me, and I knew it. I was weak and sleepy. All I could think about was my unborn daughter. I was going to miss out on her life. I knew she would be good, though. Between Trip, Ross and Murph, she wouldn't want for anything.

It was getting harder and harder to open my eyes. I wanted to go to sleep so bad, but I knew I might never wake up. It was crazy because I really wasn't scared. You were born to die; nobody was going to live forever. I found that out at a young age. I was going to hell, and I knew it, but I had planned on robbing the devil anyway.

"Don't let him close his eyes," Mr. C said.

"Keep your eyes open, Face, the ambulance is almost here," T-Mack said.

He wasn't talking about shit; my body was hurting. I closed my eyes, and welcomed the rest.

Chapter Twenty-Five

I woke up in a hospital bed with tubes everywhere! I had tubes in my chest, mouth, and side, I even had a tube in my manhood! The tube in my mouth going down my throat was making me gag. The EKG machine I was hooked up to started going off because I was panicking. I wanted the tube out of my throat.

"Oh my God! Baby, calm down." Angie ran in the room. "Doctor Jones! Mr. Lowe is awake!" she yelled.

Angie rubbed my face, trying to soothe me, but it wasn't working. The tube down my throat was debilitating.

"No! No!" the doctor said when she came in and saw that I was trying to sit up. "You have to relax, Mr. Lowe, and I'll be able to remove the feeding tube."

I wasn't trying to hear none of that! The tube was about to come out of my mouth right now! I moved my right arm and almost passed out from the pain. My right arm was in a sling, something I hadn't noticed.

"I need help in Room Twenty-One!" the doctor yelled.

"No, I got him," Angie said, as two burly nurses came in the room.

"I need you guys to restrain him while I remove the feeding tube," the doctor told the two nurses who had just come in.

"If y'all do that, you'll be dead before the sun comes back up." Trip walked into the room followed by Murph.

"Please relax, baby, and we gon' get the tube out but we can't do it with you doing all this moving," Angie tried calming me down. I laid still, and the doctor grabbed the tube and slowly pulled it out. Angie put a cup of crushed ice to my lips and said: "Go slow, don't overdo it."

The ice felt good to my raw throat. The doctor started poking and prodding me, asking a bunch of questions.

"Mr. Lowe, you're extremely lucky. You took five rounds from a .357 at close range and you're still with us. Your right arm and wrist are fractured and you lost a piece of your liver, but it's not going to prevent you from living a normal life. Your lungs healed up last month—"

I put my left hand to stop her.

"What you mean last month?" I said, barely above a whisper. I sounded like Vito from *The Godfather*.

"Bro, you were in a coma, it's March," Trip said.

That meant I had been in a coma for two months! "Take the rest of these tubes out so I can go," I whispered, laying my head back on the pillow. I was bone-tired.

"Mr. Lowe, you can't leave yet, there's still tests I need to run."

"Lady, I understand you have a job to do, but he wasn't asking you; he was telling you!" Murph spoke up.

She looked from him to me, and saw we were dead serious.

"Nurse Curtis, can I speak to you for a minute?" she asked Angie who had been rubbing my arm, trying to keep me calm the entire time. They stepped out in the hallway, and Murph went in.

"Nigga, you a bitch! You let some fuck nigga catch you lacking. Psst! Then you almost died with your gun in reach at that. What the fuck wrong with this nigga, Trip?"

"Bra, the whole first month you were in that coma we kept it hot on Rude Boy and anybody associated with him. With football season over, I been coming down here every week trying to toe-tag shit. That nigga slicker than a can of oil though because we can't catch him. Cynthia beat that nigga babymama up so bad I thought she had killed her. And she showed us where he stayed, but he ain't been going there. I went to sleep out that bitch waiting for him to show up." Trip gave me some info.

"T-Mack say you got a good look at the nigga so who was it?" Murph asked.

I shrugged, and pain shot through my body. My throat hurt when I tried to talk, so I wasn't about to say anything. I was trying to process everything. Something was telling me Rude Boy didn't have a hand in me getting shot. He had me dead to right not even two hours earlier, so why wait? It was something I was missing.

"Look at my bae!" Cynthia rushed in the room, and jumped her pregnant ass on me, causing me to cry out in pain. "I'm sorry, baby." She got up.

Cynthia was looking good as hell, big stomach and all.

"When are you due?" I croaked.

"In fifteen weeks," she beamed.

The doctor came in with Angie, and said they were going to take the tubes out, and that I needed to sign a waiver saying I was refusing treatment. Angie stroked my face, and Cynthia balled her face up.

"Excuse you," Cynthia said.

I shook my head at her, trying to kill the issue before it got out of hand.

"What?" Angie looked Cynthia up and down.

"You rubbing on my nigga face and shit."

"Oh, Face is your man?" Angie smirked. "You ain't got nothing to worry about. I'm his homegirl Angela."

"Oh, okay."

Angie tried to walk out, but I grabbed her hand and we locked eyes. Words weren't needed; she knew she was still my boo. I let her hand go, and she walked out. Just when I thought shit couldn't get any more awkward, Diqueena walked in my room, followed by a pregnant Rai'chell! She was so big her due date had to be soon.

"I'm glad you're okay," Diqueena said as she came over to my bed with the flowers she had. My room was so packed with balloons, flowers and shit that she had nowhere to put them anyway.

"People were trying to say you were dead, but I knew better. I said my brother not going out like that, and I fucked Kameesha up at school the other day too."

I scowled and whispered, "What the fuck you fighting for?"

"Oh, you don't know yet?" she asked.

"Know what?" Trip asked.

"Wait, let me talk to him first," Rai'chell spoke up. She waddled over to my bedside. "How you been?"

I looked at my body, then up at her.

"Yeah, I know. Dumb question, right? At least you're alive, Nymel."

I reached my left arm out, and touched her stomach, questioning her with my eyes.

Rai'chell smiled sadly, shook her head, and said: "Jaden." My temperature shot through the roof! I didn't know why, but I was madder than a woman stuck in the rain with a new sew-in.

Rai'chell knew it because she switched places with Diqueena.

"I know who shot you and why," she said.

I narrowed my eyes, urging her on.

"Kameesha's brother Ghost. She was walking around school bragging that her brother had got her some get back for the weight room incident."

"Don't nobody touch her, she's mine," I said.

I hit the call button for the nurse. I had to get the tubes out of me. It was time for me to go.

Chapter Twenty-Six

Any plans I had of getting right into the fold were put on hold by the way my body was feeling. After all the tubes were removed, I was released even though the doctor was strongly against it. I tried walking, but collapsed on the floor. It felt like a thousand needles were poking my legs simultaneously. I had to leave the hospital in a wheelchair. I had initially planned on staying at the house across the river, but my mama kicked against it. She said I had to bring my ass home or else! I wasn't tripping, I knew at my mom's house I would get a lot of TLC especially with Trip off to college. I didn't plan on being down long, and the doctor said my arm would be good in another week. I just had to get my muscles back to being used.

Since my mom's house had gotten shot up, me and Trip had moved her to the suburbs. We got her a white and yellow two-story house in Gates Four. I had my stuff put in the bonus room above the garage. That way, I could sneak Cynthia and Angie in without my mom knowing. Cynthia was in the bed with me, rubbing my chest, when she said "Okay now, baby, we need to come up with a name for the club."

She had been on me about the club the whole two days I had been home. Naming the club was the only thing left to do, she had already got it remodeled and everything. She showed me the club via a video she had made. The color scheme was pink, black and white. As soon as you walked in, there was a long pink couch to your left where customers could sit. Then it opened up to the main floor where mirrors adorned all the walls and the ceiling. In the middle of the floor was the main stage which was illuminated by pink lights. There were two side stages, one on each side of the club. Under the main stage there was a pull-out pool that Cynthia had installed for wet and wild Wednesdays. There were three VIP rooms, all of which had pink and black wrap around sectionals, their own bar and stripper pole.

The platform bar sat off to the right. The ten private rooms were located behind a pink curtain in the back. Each room had a pink and black couch situated up against the wall facing the door. My office, as Cynthia liked to call it, was in the back, up a set of winding steps, or you could use the elevator. The office looked down on the entire club. The windows lining the office were one-way mirrors. Looking up towards the office, all you would see would be your reflection. I couldn't lie, Cynthia had done her thing, I was thoroughly impressed.

"How about *Pleasure's Paradise*?"

"That has a nice ring to it." She put the tip of her acrylic nail in her mouth. "I like it! There's one more thing you have to do, and I specifically left it for you to do."

"What?"

"You have to hire the dancers, bartenders and bottle girls."

"Oh yeah, I'm with that." I smiled.

"I bet you are!" Cynthia rolled her eyes. "Baby, I thought I had lost you." Her eyes watered.

"But you didn't so don't start that crying shit," I warned.

"I can't help it. You're my better half. I can't live without you." Cynthia put her head on my chest.

"Bae, I'm not going anywhere anytime soon. So don't worry your pretty self. Just focus on making sure my daughter gets here safe and sound."

"Okay, daddy," she said, and we went to sleep in each other's arms.

***

After a week of rehab, I was able to get around on my own, but I had to take breaks frequently. No matter how much I tried, nobody would let me be alone; whether it was my mom, Angie, Cynthia or Murph. When Trip came down for the weekend, he would be on the same type of time. They were acting like I was a handicap, and it was starting to irk me. Even Corrigan's pussy ass was trying to carry me. I called him, asking for a folder, and he told me to wait until I was full strength.

Huh! I was far from hurting, but I wanted 100 million. When I got 100 million dollars I would leave the streets alone. I was about to show everybody that I wasn't a handicap. I put some black Levi's on and a black t-shirt. It took me ten minutes to get the shirt over my head, and another ten to get my arms through. My body still hurt, but at least I could feel pain. I could be dead. I put a pair of black 4's on, and grabbed my pistol. I crept out the house, careful not to wake Angie up, and got in the new BMW Angie had. Before I could crank the car up, someone tapped on the window, scaring me and making me draw down all at the same time. I looked out, and saw Murph's smiling face.

"Bra, you almost got dome checked. And what the fuck you doing outside my mama house at eleven o'clock at night?" I opened the door, and got out.

"I know you, nigga, and I knew it was only a matter of time before you got on your bullshit. I'm here to make sure you don't get your cripple ass killed. Now come on, let's get in my shit."

We got in his dark blue Challenger, and cruised off.

"Where were you going?" Murph questioned.

"To find Kameesha," I admitted.

"So you know where she stay at?"

"No, but I was going to find out."

Murph passed me a fat blunt, and a piece of paper with an address on it. I took two pulls of the blunt, and started coughing my lungs up.

"Slow down, nigga," he laughed.

The weed immediately took effect, my eyes got low and red. I was feeling good and mellow.

"Whose address is this?"

"Kameesha's and you'll never guess where I got it." Murph cut his eyes at me, and grinned.

"Who?" I wanted to know.

"Your boo thang Laci," he said, and started laughing so hard tears started coming out his eyes.

"Go 'head man," I laughed.

"I can't cap though, she fuck with you. When she found out you were out the hospital, she reached out to me on the book and gave me Kameesha's address, then she told me I had better handle that.

I chuckled. Let me find out Laci not only had some good sex but was also a G. I was going to have to hit her up and holler at her. I looked at the address again, and realized Kameesha stayed in Oakdale apartments.

"Murph, I'm about to do this bitch so dirty, it's gon' be sad. And then I'm gon' drag her brother, literally."

"You know I'm with the shits."

"Say no more." I took a few more pulls of the blunt, and leaned back, listening to Kevin Gates rap through the speakers. We pulled into Oakdale apartments, and parked in front of Kameesha's apartment. I got mad thinking about how Kameesha had almost got me taken out the game all because she was a slut. We got out, and walked up to her door. I knocked, and covered the peep hole. I don't know why people do it, but I learned that when you covered the peep hole, people tended to just open the door. This time proved no different. An older lady with the same high yellow complexion as Kameesha answered the door, and I punched her in the mouth, dropping her. I stepped past her, and walked up the stairs while Murph tied her up.

"Girl, that nigga been blowing my phone up trying to get some more of this mouth," Kameesha was lying on her stomach, talking on the phone.

I walked in her room, straddled her back, snatched the phone, and threw it against the wall.

"Get the fuck off me!" she yelled, and I hit her in the back of the head with my Sig.

"Scream again, bitch and I'm gon' end you right now!" I said through gritted teeth. I was hurting like hell.

I got up off the bed when Murph walked in. Kameesha turned over, and her eyes got huge upon seeing me.

"Face, I didn't tell him to do it, I swear! I had let it go but Ghost didn't." Kameesha's pleas fell on deaf ears.

"You about to call that nigga over here right now, bitch, and if you say something to tip him off you'll die in the worse way possible!" Murph warned.

"Okay," she said, and I handed her her phone. *"Ghost, something is wrong with mama! You need to get here.* He said he on his way."

I grabbed some zip ties from Murph, and tied her to the bed, spread-eagled.

"Please, Face," she begged, and I stuffed a sock that was on the bed in her mouth.

The pain that was shooting through my body was her fault, so I had to make sure she felt my pain. I went into the bathroom and grabbed a bottle of baby oil. I went downstairs, and passed Kameesha's mom who was hog-tied on the couch with a scarf stuffed in her mouth. I went in the kitchen, found a Tupperware bowl, and poured the entire bottle of baby oil in it. I put the bowl in the microwave and set the timer for three minutes. I grabbed a knife, and went back out into the living room.

Their mother looked up at me, pleading with her eyes, but I had no sympathy for her. If she hadn't had Kameesha or Ghost, I would have never gotten shot. I didn't do her dirty, though I stuck the knife through her throat. I left her to bleed out while I went to go check on the baby oil. The baby oil was bubbling up, letting me know it was ready. I grabbed a dish towel, and used it to take the bowl out of the microwave. I carefully walked up the stairs, and into Kameesha's room. I started at her feet, and worked my way up, pouring the piping hot baby oil all over her body. Everywhere the oil touched, her skin would peel all the way down to the white meat. All Kameesha had on were a pair of green boy shorts and a bra, so ninety percent of her body was exposed. She was jerking her arms and legs so hard the skin on her wrists and ankles had broken open. Her screams were being muffled by the sock in her mouth.

"Bitch, you shell." Murph looked at Kameesha's body, and the way her skin was continuing to peel.

"She shell for thinking her bad deeds were going to go un-punished," I said, throwing the rest of the baby oil in her face.

She jerked a few times, and laid still. I knew she wasn't dead because her chest was still rising and falling. "Oh shit! Her eyebrows came off!" Murph pointed out. Kameesha's entire body had turned a pinkish, reddish color. Her outer layer of skin was completely gone.

"Come on, I'm trying to handle this hoe ass nigga and go home. I need a Percocet."

We had started walking down the steps when the front door opened. Ghost saw us, and immediately started letting off. *Boom! Boom! Boom!* He let off three quick shots, striking the wall by my head, and ran back out the door. I couldn't run, so Murph ran past me out the door. When I finally did make it out the door, they were shooting it out. They were each behind cars, one would pop up and shoot, making the other one duck down, then they would trade places. Ghost was behind a Camaro off to my right. I had thirty in the clip of my Sig, so I started walking down on him, shooting the Sig. Murph saw what I was doing, and followed suit. Ghost came up to shoot, and his gun jammed again. Oh my! They say God blessing all the trap niggas, but he blessing the jackboys too. Ghost tried to run, and Murph shot him in the leg.

"Tie him up and put him in the trunk," I said.

I went back in Kameesha's, and up the steps. I put three rounds in Kameesha, and walked out.

Several police cars passed us on our way to the house on the eastside, so I could get my truck. I got my truck and headed to Hope Mills. I had stumbled on a big open field one day when I had made the wrong turn; that's where we were headed. We got Ghost out the trunk, made a slipknot out of the thick rope I had, and put it around his feet. The other end of the rope I tied to the back of my truck. Ghost started fighting and yelling when he saw what he was in store for. I got behind the wheel and took off. The field was about a football field long, and two football fields wide. I planned on making him touch every blade of grass out there. I drove around the field at high speeds for five minutes straight. When I stopped and got out to inspect my work, I stepped on his arm; it wasn't connected to his body. Ghost was unrecognizable! Both of his legs were bent in angles that your legs weren't supposed to go. The skin on his face was gone. The left side of his face was only bone, even his eye was gone on that side.

"Gotdamn!" Murph walked over and said.

"Fuck 'em"

179

I cut the rope, gave my day one a half hug, and went home. I needed to rest; my body was hurting so bad I felt like I was going to pass out.

Angie was up waiting on me when I walked in. She was about to go in on me until she saw how much pain I was in. She helped me up the stairs, and into bed. I popped two Percocet pills, and passed out.

Chapter Twenty-Seven

I rounded all my niggas up, and took them to *Pleasure's Paradise* with me. It was me, Murph, Ross, Sha Loc and Tyrone. Trip hadn't come down this week. I had to get Cynthia off my back about the club; she was making it seem like I was the one holding the grand opening up. So me and my boys were about to pick the strippers.

"I see you all healed up," Sha Loc said.

"For the most part," I said, taking a seat on the pink couch, facing the main stage.

I still wasn't a hundred percent, but I could move around without having to sit down every so often.

"Where the drinks at?" Murph asked.

"Where the hoes at?" Sha Loc countered.

"Fuck that, where the loud at?" Tyrone added.

"Nigga, you see Murph over there rolling up." I shook my head. It had been a while since we had all gotten together and kicked it, something we used to do all the time.

I looked up, and there were women piling through the door. I got up to greet them.

"How you pretty ladies doing?" I asked them, motioning for them to follow me.

I led them to the dressing room in the back under my office.

The dressing room was all pink with twenty-five separate stations that came with white dressers and pink chairs so all the dancers would have their own station to do their make-up and outfits. There were full mirrors on every wall. The carpet in the dressing room was pink with white P's all over it. There was also a huge walk-in shower around the back, where they could shower if need be.

"Who's going first? And when are we going to know if we're getting hired or not?" a thick brown-skinned girl asked.

"That's for y'all to decide, and you'll know before you leave if you're going to have a spot or not. I want those of you who are applying for the bartender and bottle girl spots to come with me. The required outfits for the bartenders and bottle girls are hanging up over there." I pointed.

The outfits consisted of black boy shorts with a pink P on each cheek, or they could wear the black leggings with *Pleasure's* on one leg and *Paradise* on the other. The shirts were pink halter tops with black P's all over the front. Once hired, each girl's name would be on the back.

I counted thirty women of varying shapes, sizes and colors.

"Are we late?" Pocahontas came in with ten beautiful women trailing her.

"Nah, but you know you don't have to audition—I already have a spot for you," I informed her. "I need all the bartenders and bottle girls to come with me."

They were going to be making our drinks because I sho' nuff wasn't going to be doing it. I walked out, went to the DJ booth, and cut on a playlist I made for the club, and went and sat down. I grabbed the blunt from Ross, and took three long pulls. The potent weed instantly sent me to Pluto! I sunk down in the cushion, as the bartenders and bottle girls came out. There were ten of them, and all of them looked edible in their booty shorts. Of the ten, eight were black, and the other two were a Chinese beauty and a white girl with burgundy hair. All of them were thick with the exception of the snow bunny; she had a tight little butt, but had some 36 DD's. And she was runway-model-sexy. She had her hair in two braids that hung to her ass.

"What are you drinking on?" the white chick walked up on me and asked.

"Bring me a bottle of Patron," I told her.

I watched as she walked away. Shorty was about 5'9, with some long legs. The black boy shorts hugged her petite frame perfectly, giving her booty a nice lift. Of the 140 pounds she probably weighed, forty of it came from the DD's she had on her chest. Her eyes were her most intriguing feature; they were purple with yellow specks. She turned around, and caught me staring at her ass, and smirked. *Cynthia was going to fire her*, I thought to myself.

I turned from the white girl, as one of the girls Pocahontas had brought with her came out onto the stage. She was stacked like a brick house! She stood 5'0, with honey blond hair that hung to the middle of her back, and was about 165 pounds, endowed breasts and ass that moved with every step she took. Her pecan brown complexion was a nice compliment to her soft brown eyes.

"Your name?" I looked through the pile of applications I had.

"Danielle—My stage name is Brown Sugar," she replied.

"Go ahead and handle your business."

Brown Sugar threw her yellow bra in Tyrone's lap, and climbed the twenty foot pole, using only her legs! She got to the top, and twerked her way back to the bottom. *I'm in Love With a Stripper* played in the background, as she removed the yellow G-string, and tossed it on the stage, revealing a set of eyes that sat on each side of her clit.

"Danielle, you can stop," I said.

"Stop? It was just getting good!" Sha Loc said.

"Danielle, you can tell Pocahontas and all the girls she brought with her that they don't have to audition."

I knew from Danielle's audition that Pocahontas had brought straight money makers with her, so it was no need to see the other nine. I was more than sure of their pedigree.

She smiled, and walked backstage.

"Aye, man, you can't be stopping them in the middle of their act," Ross said with a handful of money.

"Chill, trick, it's plenty more in the back. I need to see the girls that aren't already a pro. She was a vet so why waste time? So sit back and relax."

"Y'all know that nigga be super thirsty," Murph laughed, grabbing the butt of one of the bottle girls, as she sat a gold bottle at the table.

It looked like the bartenders and bottle girls were keepers. R. Kelly's *Half on a Baby* came on, and a honey colored beauty sashayed on stage in a school girl get up. Her kinky brown hair was done in two pigtails. Her white button up shirt was tied in a knot, showcasing her flat stomach. It was unbuttoned; so with every step she took, her C cups would play peek-a-boo. The blue checkered mini she wore came to the bottom of her ass cheeks, giving us a glimpse of the white thong hiding between her legs.

"Your name?" I asked.

"Baby Doll," she said, and started her set.

She turned her back to us, and bent over, taking the miniskirt off, all the while swaying to the beat. Baby Doll let the mini fall around her feet, and placed her hands flat on the stage, and started popping her ass one cheek at a time. This earned her a shower of ones from Ross. I was disinterested. I had seen enough, but I wasn't going to rain on my boys parade. I had brought them so they could have a good time.

I got up, and was walking to my office when Pocahontas and the girls she had brought with her came out the back.

"Where you going?" Pocahontas stopped me.

"To my office to chill and look over some paperwork."

"I thought you were supposed to be watching the auditions, you can't do that from your office" an outrageously thick chocolate girl with a 40-inch lime green wig said.

I actually could, but I didn't have to tell her that.

"Dizzy, he one of them funny style niggas—He don't believe in throwing money on a woman he's not screwing," Pocahontas said.

"Is that right?" the girl Dizzy asked.

"I don't get nothing out of it but a hard dick, but I can call my bitch, and she gon' strip, suck and fuck for free," I said.

"Oh, it don't be free—You pay her bills, buy her clothes or something," a yellowbone with a hot pink wig said.

"That's not the same. It's different when I'm outright throwing you some money for a lap dance. I might as well go to Backpage and buy some pussy."

"Ain't nothing wrong with paying for sex," a petite chick said.

"So you don't respect the hustle?" Brown Sugar narrowed her eyes.

I smiled. "Well, as long as you're not looking to make a career out of it. There's no such thing as a retirement check from strippers." I didn't even know where the words were coming from. "Besides, if I didn't respect the hustle, I wouldn't be opening the club."

"You're the owner? I thought you were just the manager or something," Dizzy said with lust and greed in her eyes.

"Down, girl. Cynthia would kill you!" Pocahontas intervened. "Tell her to call me too." She led her crew out the glass doors, looking like a stack of new blue faces.

We didn't get through with all the auditions until nine that night. We would've been done, but girls kept showing up trying to earn a spot. I could already tell we were about to put the club game in the headlock. We were already opening the biggest strip club in the city at 14,000 square feet, but we were going to have the baddest dancers, bottle girls and bartenders. I got in my Audi R8, and headed to Cynthia's. She hadn't been answering her phone, so I knew she was in her feelings about something.   Nothing some good sex and a new clutch wouldn't solve. I turned YFN Lucci's song: "All Night Long" on because after all that ass and pussy at the club, I was about to be in her guts all night long. As I pulled onto the road leading to her apartment complex, a red beamer shot past me, running the red light.

"Was that Rude Boy's car?" I asked myself, speeding through the guard gate.

I hopped out, leaving my door open, and rushing up to Cynthia's apartment. I was about to let her know that I wasn't the one to be playing games with. If she wanted to be with somebody else, then that's what it was. Her apartment door was cracked open when I got to it. A smell I knew all too well assaulted my nose—The coppery smell of blood.

"Cynthia!" I yelled, hoping for a response.

I slow-walked down the hallway until I got to the bedroom. Cynthia was sprawled out in the middle of the bed in a pool of blood.

"Baby!" I grabbed her limp body into my arms, then I thought about our baby.

I looked down, and noticed her stomach had been cut open

.

"What the fuck!" I called 911

Rude Boy had killed Cynthia, and cut my baby out of her belly. I couldn't really talk. My emotions were all over the place. Rude Boy had taken it to new levels. For this he had to die in the most heinous way possible.

Wait a minute! Where was my baby? I laid Cynthia down, and looked around. I walked into the bathroom and threw up. Rude Boy had hung my baby from the shower rail by her umbilical cord.

"I'm gon' kill this nigga, yo," I whispered, as tears fell from my eyes.

"Freeze! Don't move!" a white cop yelled.

"I'm the one who called the ambulance, stupid!" I snapped.

"Hands! Let me see your hands!" he yelled, turning red.

I thought of how the police had been killing unarmed black men and getting away with it, and bit back my smart remark. I put my hands on my head, and got on my knees. He slung me to the ground, and cuffed me. The paramedics rushed by us on our way to the patrol car. Red Beard was pulling into the parking lot, as I was put in the backseat. Red Beard talked to the cop and came over to me.

"Before you say anything, I stay here. I'm the one who called 911."

"Hold tight," he walked over.

A minute later, he came back and let me out.

I called Cynthia's mom, and told her what was going on. She said they were on the way, before I was done talking. The homicide detectives showed up, and asked me a bunch of dumb questions; then when they got done, Cynthia's parents showed up. Cynthia's mom passed out when they wheeled Cynthia's body past. Cynthia's dad walked up to me and said, "You better find out who did this to my baby girl and make them pay."

I nodded and walked away. I called Murph. We were about to paint the city red.

Nicholas Lock

Chapter Twenty-Eight

There wasn't a penny being made in Taylors Creek! It had been five days since Cynthia had been killed, and somebody had lost their life every day. I crept through 301 every single day and blew smoke! Anybody I caught at or by one of Rude Boy's traps were a shot ass! Yesterday, I had tried to gun his baby mama and their teenage daughter down, but I missed. Nobody was exempt! I was in the process of finding out where his mother stayed.

"What's popping, nigga?" Murph came into the living room, wearing a black suit.

"Murder," I said, loading bullets into the drum I had recently bought.

"Today is Cynthia's funeral, nigga! You forgot?"

I had totally forgotten! Killing Rude Boy was my sole purpose in life at the moment. I didn't know how much I truly loved Cynthia until she was taken from me. Cynthia had become my better half, my voice of reason when I was on the edge. She really had me thinking about living a long life when, before, I was content with making it to twenty-one. Rude Boy had taken all of that, so now he was going to feel the wrath of a nigga who didn't give a fuck about life. I grabbed the bottle of E&J I was drinking, and went to change. I looked in my closet, and pulled out a pair of Dolce & Gabbana jeans, a black Gucci button-up and some black Kobe 11s. I was thugging, my baby wouldn't trip. She knew how I was. Murph could only shake his head when he saw my outfit. I rode with Murph in his red Aston Martin. The whole ride all I kept playing was T.I's *Live in the Sky*.

Lewis Chapel was packed full for my baby's funeral. When we got out, I was surprised to see my twin, Ross, Sha Loc and Tyrone all dressed in black designer suits. We walked in the church, and they all took seats in the back, but I stayed standing. After a few minutes, I started making my way to the front. I couldn't stop looking at the two caskets. Cynthia's was white and gold, and my baby's was pink and white. Cynthia's was the only one open. I laid my hand on Cynthia's hand, and said: "I'm sorry I wasn't there to protect you and our baby, but I'm gon' make it up to you. There's so much I want to say to you, but you know I'm not good at this sort of thing. So just make sure you holler at God and ask him to forgive me for the sins I'm about to commit." I kissed Cynthia's forehead, both eyes and her lips, and walked out the church.

I needed to make someone bleed.

"Mr. Lowe. Keep your hands where I can see them." There were about twenty police cars scattered around the parking lot. In my confusion they rushed me, and tossed me on the ground. A detective stood over me and said, "You're under arrest for the murders of Sarah Thompson, Karl Thompson, and the attempted murder of Kameesha Thompson."

Chapter Twenty-Nine

I had been locked up for a month in the Cumberland County Jail with no bond. Kameesha had a guardian angel because I know I had shot her at point-blank range, but she had lived. I wasn't tripping because I knew one of my niggas would handle her soon. I was on my way to court for my first appearance. COVID-19 was turning the world upside down, so the court schedule varied day to day.

"What you think they about to do?" Ox asked me.

I had met Ox in the county. We were in the same high bond block. He was locked up for banging out with the police.

"Not shit but give me a continuance—A waste of time," I said. "The only reason I came was to see some hoes."

"All them hoes that came to see you, ain't no way you want to see more."

"Shitting me."

"Lowe, come on!" the sheriff yelled.

I walked out the holding cell, and followed him to courtroom 2B. My case hadn't been bound over to superior court, so I was still in district court. The first faces I saw when I walked in the courtroom was Rai'chell and Diqueena's. They smiled and waved. Diqueena came to all my court dates, but this was Rai'chell's first time coming. We had been writing each other for the last few weeks, but she never said anything about coming to my court date. I looked at Diqueena, and she kept cutting her eyes at Rai'chell. I didn't know what Diqueena had going on; she was always being goofy. But as I got to the defense table, I saw Rai'chell had a baby boy in her lap, and he looked exactly like me! Before I could ask her what was good, the Bailiff yelled: "All rise for the honorable Judge Weeks!"

Judge Weeks? I turned to see Cynthia's dad taking a seat on the bench. We locked eyes for a brief second, and he winked.

To Be Continued...

Confessions of a Jackboy 2

Coming Soon

Submission Guideline

Submit the first three chapters of your completed manuscript to <u>ldpsubmissions@gmail.com</u>, subject line: Your book's title. The manuscript must be in a .doc file and sent as an attachment. Document should be in Times New Roman, double spaced and in size 12 font. Also, provide your synopsis and full contact information. If sending multiple submissions, they must each be in a separate email.

Have a story but no way to send it electronically? You can still submit to LDP/Ca$h Presents. Send in the first three chapters, written or typed, of your completed manuscript to:

LDP: Submissions Dept
Po Box 944
Stockbridge, Ga 30281

DO NOT send original manuscript. Must be a duplicate.

Provide your synopsis and a cover letter containing your full contact information.

Thanks for considering LDP and Ca$h Presents.

Nicholas Lock

**<u>Coming Soon from Lock Down Publications/Ca$h Pre-
sents</u>**

BOW DOWN TO MY GANGSTA

By **Ca$h**

TORN BETWEEN TWO

By **Coffee**

BLOOD OF A BOSS **VI**

SHADOWS OF THE GAME II

TRAP BASTARD II

By **Askari**

LOYAL TO THE GAME **IV**

By **T.J. & Jelissa**

IF LOVING YOU IS WRONG… **III**

By **Jelissa**

TRUE SAVAGE **VIII**

MIDNIGHT CARTEL IV

DOPE BOY MAGIC IV

CITY OF KINGZ III

By **Chris Green**

BLAST FOR ME **III**

A SAVAGE DOPEBOY III

CUTTHROAT MAFIA III

DUFFLE BAG CARTEL VII

HEARTLESS GOON VI

By **Ghost**

A HUSTLER'S DECEIT III

KILL ZONE **II**

BAE BELONGS TO ME III

A DOPE BOY'S QUEEN III

By **Aryanna**

COKE KINGS V

KING OF THE TRAP III

By **T.J. Edwards**

GORILLAZ IN THE BAY V

3X KRAZY III

De'Kari

THE STREETS ARE CALLING II

Duquie Wilson

KINGPIN KILLAZ IV

STREET KINGS III

PAID IN BLOOD III

CARTEL KILLAZ IV

DOPE GODS III

Hood Rich

SINS OF A HUSTLA II

ASAD

KINGZ OF THE GAME VI

Playa Ray

SLAUGHTER GANG IV

RUTHLESS HEART IV

By Willie Slaughter

FUK SHYT II

By Blakk Diamond

Nicholas Lock

TRAP QUEEN

RICH $AVAGE II

MONEY IN THE GRAVE II

By Troublesome

YAYO V

GHOST MOB II

Stilloan Robinson

CREAM III

By Yolanda Moore

SON OF A DOPE FIEND III

HEAVEN GOT A GHETTO II

By Renta

FOREVER GANGSTA II

GLOCKS ON SATIN SHEETS III

By Adrian Dulan

LOYALTY AIN'T PROMISED III

By Keith Williams

THE PRICE YOU PAY FOR LOVE III

By Destiny Skai

I'M NOTHING WITHOUT HIS LOVE II

SINS OF A THUG II

TO THE THUG I LOVED BEFORE II

By Monet Dragun

LIFE OF A SAVAGE IV

MURDA SEASON IV

GANGLAND CARTEL IV

CHI'RAQ GANGSTAS IV

196

KILLERS ON ELM STREET IV

JACK BOYZ N DA BRONX III

A DOPEBOY'S DREAM II

By **Romell Tukes**

QUIET MONEY IV

EXTENDED CLIP III

THUG LIFE IV

By **Trai'Quan**

THE STREETS MADE ME III

By **Larry D. Wright**

IF YOU CROSS ME ONCE II

ANGEL III

By **Anthony Fields**

FRIEND OR FOE III

By **Mimi**

SAVAGE STORMS III

By **Meesha**

THE STREETS WILL NEVER CLOSE II

By **K'ajji**

IN THE ARM OF HIS BOSS

By **Jamila**

HARD AND RUTHLESS III

MOB TOWN 251 II

By **Von Diesel**

LEVELS TO THIS SHYT II

By **Ah'Million**

MOB TIES III

By SayNoMore

FOR THE LOVE OF A BOSS III

By C. D. Blue

MOBBED UP II

By King Rio

BRED IN THE GAME II

By S. Allen

KILLA KOUNTY II

By Khufu

CONFESSIONS OF A JACKBOY II

By Nicholas Lock

Available Now

RESTRAINING ORDER **I & II**

By **CA$H & Coffee**

LOVE KNOWS NO BOUNDARIES **I II & III**

By **Coffee**

RAISED AS A GOON I, II, III & IV

BRED BY THE SLUMS I, II, III

BLAST FOR ME I & II

ROTTEN TO THE CORE I II III

A BRONX TALE I, II, III

DUFFLE BAG CARTEL I II III IV V VI

HEARTLESS GOON I II III IV V

A SAVAGE DOPEBOY I II

DRUG LORDS I II III

CUTTHROAT MAFIA I II

By **Ghost**

LAY IT DOWN **I & II**

LAST OF A DYING BREED I II

BLOOD STAINS OF A SHOTTA I & II III

By **Jamaica**

LOYAL TO THE GAME I II III

LIFE OF SIN I, II III

By **TJ & Jelissa**

BLOODY COMMAS I & II

SKI MASK CARTEL I II & III

KING OF NEW YORK I II,III IV V

RISE TO POWER I II III

COKE KINGS I II III IV

BORN HEARTLESS I II III IV

KING OF THE TRAP I II

By **T.J. Edwards**

IF LOVING HIM IS WRONG…I & II

LOVE ME EVEN WHEN IT HURTS I II III

By **Jelissa**

WHEN THE STREETS CLAP BACK I & II III

THE HEART OF A SAVAGE I II III

By **Jibril Williams**

Nicholas Lock

A DISTINGUISHED THUG STOLE MY HEART I II & III

LOVE SHOULDN'T HURT I II III IV

RENEGADE BOYS I II III IV

PAID IN KARMA I II III

SAVAGE STORMS I II

AN UNFORESEEN LOVE

By **Meesha**

A GANGSTER'S CODE I &, II III

A GANGSTER'S SYN I II III

THE SAVAGE LIFE I II III

CHAINED TO THE STREETS I II III

BLOOD ON THE MONEY I II III

By J-Blunt

PUSH IT TO THE LIMIT

By **Bre' Hayes**

BLOOD OF A BOSS **I, II, III, IV, V**

SHADOWS OF THE GAME

TRAP BASTARD

By **Askari**

THE STREETS BLEED MURDER **I, II & III**

THE HEART OF A GANGSTA I II& III

By **Jerry Jackson**

CUM FOR ME I II III IV V VI VII

An **LDP Erotica Collaboration**

BRIDE OF A HUSTLA **I II & II**

THE FETTI GIRLS **I, II& III**

CORRUPTED BY A GANGSTA I, II III, IV

200

Confessions of a Jackboy

BLINDED BY HIS LOVE

THE PRICE YOU PAY FOR LOVE I II

DOPE GIRL MAGIC I II III

By **Destiny Skai**

WHEN A GOOD GIRL GOES BAD

By **Adrienne**

THE COST OF LOYALTY I II III

By Kweli

A GANGSTER'S REVENGE **I II III & IV**

THE BOSS MAN'S DAUGHTERS I II III IV V

A SAVAGE LOVE **I & II**

BAE BELONGS TO ME I II

A HUSTLER'S DECEIT I, II, III

WHAT BAD BITCHES DO I, II, III

SOUL OF A MONSTER I II III

KILL ZONE

A DOPE BOY'S QUEEN I II

By **Aryanna**

A KINGPIN'S AMBITON

A KINGPIN'S AMBITION **II**

I MURDER FOR THE DOUGH

By **Ambitious**

TRUE SAVAGE I II III IV V VI VII

DOPE BOY MAGIC I, II, III

MIDNIGHT CARTEL I II III

CITY OF KINGZ I II

By **Chris Green**

Nicholas Lock

A DOPEBOY'S PRAYER
By **Eddie "Wolf" Lee**
THE KING CARTEL **I, II & III**
By **Frank Gresham**
THESE NIGGAS AIN'T LOYAL **I, II & III**
By **Nikki Tee**
GANGSTA SHYT **I II &III**
By **CATO**
THE ULTIMATE BETRAYAL
By **Phoenix**
BOSS'N UP **I , II & III**
By **Royal Nicole**
I LOVE YOU TO DEATH
By Destiny J
I RIDE FOR MY HITTA
I STILL RIDE FOR MY HITTA
By **Misty Holt**
LOVE & CHASIN' PAPER
By **Qay Crockett**
TO DIE IN VAIN
SINS OF A HUSTLA
By **ASAD**
BROOKLYN HUSTLAZ
By **Boogsy Morina**
BROOKLYN ON LOCK I & II
By **Sonovia**
GANGSTA CITY

202

Confessions of a Jackboy

By **Teddy Duke**

A DRUG KING AND HIS DIAMOND I & II III

A DOPEMAN'S RICHES

HER MAN, MINE'S TOO I, II

CASH MONEY HO'S

THE WIFEY I USED TO BE I II

By Nicole Goosby

TRAPHOUSE KING **I II & III**

KINGPIN KILLAZ I II III

STREET KINGS I II

PAID IN BLOOD **I II**

CARTEL KILLAZ I II III

DOPE GODS I II

By **Hood Rich**

LIPSTICK KILLAH **I, II, III**

CRIME OF PASSION I II & III

FRIEND OR FOE I II

By **Mimi**

STEADY MOBBN' **I, II, III**

THE STREETS STAINED MY SOUL I II

By **Marcellus Allen**

WHO SHOT YA **I, II, III**

SON OF A DOPE FIEND I II

HEAVEN GOT A GHETTO

Renta

GORILLAZ IN THE BAY **I II III IV**

TEARS OF A GANGSTA I II

Nicholas Lock

3X KRAZY I II
DE'KARI
TRIGGADALE I II III
Elijah R. Freeman
GOD BLESS THE TRAPPERS I, II, III
THESE SCANDALOUS STREETS I, II, III
FEAR MY GANGSTA I, II, III IV, V
THESE STREETS DON'T LOVE NOBODY I, II
BURY ME A G I, II, III, IV, V
A GANGSTA'S EMPIRE I, II, III, IV
THE DOPEMAN'S BODYGAURD I II
THE REALEST KILLAZ I II III
THE LAST OF THE OGS I II III
Tranay Adams
THE STREETS ARE CALLING
Duquie Wilson
MARRIED TO A BOSS... I II III
By Destiny Skai & Chris Green
KINGZ OF THE GAME I II III IV V
Playa Ray
SLAUGHTER GANG I II III
RUTHLESS HEART I II III
By Willie Slaughter
FUK SHYT
By Blakk Diamond
DON'T F#CK WITH MY HEART I II
By Linnea

ADDICTED TO THE DRAMA I II III

IN THE ARM OF HIS BOSS II

By Jamila

YAYO I II III IV

A SHOOTER'S AMBITION I II

BRED IN THE GAME

By S. Allen

TRAP GOD I II III

RICH $AVAGE

MONEY IN THE GRAVE

By Troublesome

FOREVER GANGSTA

GLOCKS ON SATIN SHEETS I II

By Adrian Dulan

TOE TAGZ I II III

LEVELS TO THIS SHYT

By Ah'Million

KINGPIN DREAMS I II III

By Paper Boi Rari

CONFESSIONS OF A GANGSTA I II III

CONFESSIONS OF A JACKBOY

By Nicholas Lock

I'M NOTHING WITHOUT HIS LOVE

SINS OF A THUG

TO THE THUG I LOVED BEFORE

By Monet Dragun

Nicholas Lock

CAUGHT UP IN THE LIFE I II III
By Robert Baptiste
NEW TO THE GAME I II III
MONEY, MURDER & MEMORIES I II III
By **Malik D. Rice**
LIFE OF A SAVAGE I II III
A GANGSTA'S QUR'AN I II III
MURDA SEASON I II III
GANGLAND CARTEL I II III
CHI'RAQ GANGSTAS I II III
KILLERS ON ELM STREET I II III
JACK BOYZ N DA BRONX I II
A DOPEBOY'S DREAM
By **Romell Tukes**
LOYALTY AIN'T PROMISED I II
By Keith Williams
QUIET MONEY I II III
THUG LIFE I II III
EXTENDED CLIP I II
By **Trai'Quan**
THE STREETS MADE ME I II
By **Larry D. Wright**
THE ULTIMATE SACRIFICE I, II, III, IV, V, VI
KHADIFI
IF YOU CROSS ME ONCE
ANGEL I II

Confessions of a Jackboy

IN THE BLINK OF AN EYE

By **Anthony Fields**

THE LIFE OF A HOOD STAR

By **Ca$h & Rashia Wilson**

THE STREETS WILL NEVER CLOSE

By **K'ajji**

CREAM I II

By **Yolanda Moore**

NIGHTMARES OF A HUSTLA I II III

By **King Dream**

CONCRETE KILLA I II

By **Kingpen**

HARD AND RUTHLESS I II

MOB TOWN 251

By **Von Diesel**

GHOST MOB II

Stilloan Robinson

MOB TIES I II

By **SayNoMore**

BODYMORE MURDERLAND I II III

By **Delmont Player**

FOR THE LOVE OF A BOSS I II

By **C. D. Blue**

MOBBED UP

By **King Rio**

KILLA KOUNTY

By **Khufu**

<u>BOOKS BY LDP'S CEO, CA$H</u>

<u>TRUST IN NO MAN</u>

<u>TRUST IN NO MAN 2</u>

<u>TRUST IN NO MAN 3</u>

<u>BONDED BY BLOOD</u>

<u>SHORTY GOT A THUG</u>

<u>THUGS CRY</u>

<u>THUGS CRY 2</u>

<u>THUGS CRY 3</u>

<u>TRUST NO BITCH</u>

<u>TRUST NO BITCH 2</u>

<u>TRUST NO BITCH 3</u>

<u>TIL MY CASKET DROPS</u>

<u>RESTRAINING ORDER</u>

<u>RESTRAINING ORDER 2</u>

<u>IN LOVE WITH A CONVICT</u>

<u>LIFE OF A HOOD STAR</u>

Confessions of a Jackboy